"What are we going to do?" Jill asked in a tremulous voice

Jack hung his suit jacket in the hotel closet. "*I'm* going to jump in the shower. Care to join me?"

"I don't mean—" Her words came to an abrupt stop and she shot him a nervous look. "What are you doing now?" she asked as he unzipped his trousers.

"I usually get undressed before I shower. Don't you?" His trousers fell to the floor and he stepped out of them.

"Don't be cute, Jack," she snapped. "We can't have a meaningful discussion with you standing there in your boxer shorts."

He grinned. "I could take them off."

"How can you be so . . . so . . ."

"Sexy? Provocative? Roguish?" he teased. "Come on, Jill. You worry too much."

"How would you know?" Jill asked with trepidation. "We've only spent a total of six days together."

"Seven. One whole week," he replied huskily. "Happy anniversary, darling." And when he led her to bed, she knew he was in the mood to celebrate. . . .

Elise Title's sixth Temptation novel, *Jack and Jill*, is a delightful and funny variation on the theme of marriage. And Elise sure knows what she's talking about. As a social worker, she's been counseling couples for fifteen years. In fact, Elise and her husband—what better coauthor?— are writing a how-to book on the different ways to keep relationships alive and well. Obviously a source of suggestions for happy endings!

Elise is now busy working on a miniseries for Temptation in which she tells, in her usual witty fashion, the story of the four Fortune brothers—four eligible men who find out how remaining single to save their *fortune* is not necessarily the key to happiness....

Books by Elise Title

HARLEQUIN TEMPTATION

Jack and Jill
ELISE TITLE

Harlequin Books

TORONTO • NEW YORK • LONDON
AMSTERDAM • PARIS • SYDNEY • HAMBURG
STOCKHOLM • ATHENS • TOKYO • MILAN

Published August 1991

ISBN 0-373-25458-X

JACK AND JILL

Printed in U.S.A.

PART I

JACK AND JILL WENT UP THE HILL
TO FETCH A PAIL OF WATER...

1

Jack

JACK SQUINTED INTO THE bathroom mirror. To shave or not to shave, that was the question. He was four days into his vacation on the lush tropical island of Tobago. It had not begun auspiciously. He'd managed to break a lens in his only pair of glasses on the morning of his arrival at Hotel Caribe Reef, then discovered there was no optician on the island. In order to replace the lens, he would have had to send the glasses over to Trinidad, and it would take anywhere from three days to a week to get them back. He only had four more days of vacation so he didn't bother.

Without glasses, his vision wasn't all that bad. Things just weren't very sharp, particularly around the edges. Normally that disturbed him, especially at work, but here on a tropical island where he'd come for rest and relaxation before beginning a new job in a new city, he didn't actually mind seeing the world around him with softer edges. It fit his holiday mood.

Jack took stock of himself in the mirror. Not only did he have a three-day growth of stubble on his face, his hair was in need of a good trim. Back in the real world, he was a very tidy sort of person, but he kind of liked the startling contrast from his usual crisp, buttoned-down appearance. He was on vacation after all. On a tropical island. When in Rome—or Tobago, as it were . . .

So he stuck his razor back in the medicine cabinet and splashed on some cologne he'd bought for the trip. He thought it had a Caribbean sort of scent. He had to laugh, taking one last slightly out-of-focus look at his rugged face, imagining for a moment that he was Robinson Crusoe washed up on the beach of Tobago Island.

An hour later Jack was sitting alone at a table covered in cotton batik under a peppermint-striped umbrella in the hotel's patio restaurant. The patio was built on a sandy, palm-studded beach punctuated with picturesque thatched gazebos. Twenty yards or so down the soft white sand was the gin-clear sea. He was contentedly listening to the murmur of the surf, enjoying the trade-wind-fed breeze and sampling one of the local specialties, a seafood stew called callaloo, when an attractive blonde stopped at his table. She placed a thin, filter-tipped cigarette between her toffee-colored lips, leaned ever so slightly toward him, and asked if he had a light.

"Sorry, I don't smoke," he said politely.

Then he noticed the gold-covered matchbook with *Hotel Caribe Reef* embossed on it sitting in the unused ashtray on his table—sitting, he noted then, in every ashtray on every table in the restaurant.

Jack was being a bit slow on the uptake. The very attractive blonde was actually picking him up. This kind of thing didn't happen to him. He gallantly lit her cigarette, trying to look like this kind of thing happened to him all the time.

"You've got a great tan," she said through an exhale of smoke from her puckered toffee lips.

She introduced herself as Suzanne from Dayton, Ohio.

"I'm Jack." He didn't bother with the "from" part. He hadn't settled into Philly yet, but he was no longer a resident of Chicago. What did it matter where he was from, anyway?

"You know," she said through hooded eyes and another puff of smoke, "in bygone days you could have passed for a buccaneer."

Jack laughed. He thought about Robinson Crusoe again, glad he'd skipped the shave and the haircut. He couldn't say Suzanne from Dayton was exactly his type, but he couldn't say he wasn't flattered, either. He was contemplating asking her to sit down and join him for an after-dinner drink when his eyes happened to wander over to the French doors opening onto the patio. A gasp escaped his lips; his gaze stuck.

Jack Harrington was not a man given to romantic hyperbole. He never liked gushy love stories. He always changed the dial on the car radio when that dreamy mood music came on. He didn't believe in hearing bells, seeing stars, or falling in love at first sight.

But now, as he first laid eyes on Jill, a whole damn army of romantic hyperboles marched into his head. Of course, he didn't find out her name until later, but at the very first instant he saw her he knew she was the one for him. The only one. Crusoe had found his Friday on Tobago, and he had found his one true love. See, hyperbole!

She stood at the entrance, an auburn-haired beauty in a tropical-print strapless dress that blew against a body that looked like it had been designed by Michelangelo. Her thick hair fell over her creamy shoulders in careless lustrous waves. Even though his vision wasn't perfect, he knew he was looking at perfection.

As the maître d' started to lead the young woman across the patio, Jack couldn't take his eyes off her. He loved her walk, the way her hair moved with her. He couldn't believe his luck when the maître d' showed her to the empty table right next to his. All of his senses shifted into overdrive. He was captivated by the scent of her perfume as it wafted by him—a mingling of hibiscus and lime. He was electrified by the husky sound of her voice as she thanked the maître d'. He could imagine the feel of her creamy skin against his palms....

She had to be a new arrival. There was no possible way this auburn-haired goddess could have ever escaped his notice.

"It's such a lovely night," the blonde was saying to him in between puffs. "Wouldn't a moonlight stroll be nice?"

A moonlight stroll. Yes, yes, perfect, he was thinking, then realized his silent nod was giving the poor blonde the wrong idea.

"Oh, sorry. I've got . . . other plans for tonight." He did his best to keep his attention focused on the blonde, at least while he made his apology, but the flawless beauty seated less than five feet away from him kept drawing his gaze like a magnet.

The blonde stubbed out her cigarette in his ashtray, gave him a churlish nod and took off.

His goddess had to know he was staring at her. He knew it was rude, that he was acting the absolute fool, but some unnamed force held him riveted. She finally looked his way.

He smiled a little crookedly at her, hoping it came off making him look rugged and not like a lovesick idiot, which would have been a direct mirror of his inner feelings.

She smiled back. A simple nod of acknowledgment would have pleased and even encouraged him, but her smile, her glorious smile, bowled him over.

His goddess went back to perusing the menu. Just before the waitress approached her table for her order, he boldly leaned toward her.

"You should try the callaloo. It's made with local seafood. Very tasty." He tried hard to give it his best buccaneer drawl, but even he heard the quiver of excitement and anticipation in his voice.

She lowered her gaze in a demure and utterly beguiling fashion as she bestowed another smile on him.

"Thanks for the suggestion." That husky Marilyn Monroe voice drove him wild.

When the waitress came over to her table, to his delight, she ordered the callaloo.

"Delight" was an understatement. He was delirious. Oh, not just because she ordered the callaloo, not just because of her looks, her smile, her unbelievably sexy voice. But because she was the one. Because as soon as she stepped into his view, she took up permanent residence in this empty space inside of him that he'd only just realized was there. Now even the air around him had changed. It was thicker, lusher, more intense.

His outlook on his quiet, restful vacation immediately altered. No longer was he thinking about sublime relaxation—contemplative sails, finishing up that intrigue novel he'd begun on the flight in, lying alone on the white sand, soaking up the sun, making plans about work and organizing in his head the projects he meant to do in his new apartment. Now it was impossible for him to see beyond her.

Impulsively, even though he was almost finished with his callaloo, he invited her to join him.

"Since we're both alone . . ." He said it with a partial question mark. Was she here alone or was her lover too weary from the trip in to come down for dinner? Jack was sure his heart literally stopped until she said, "Yes, I guess we are. I guess...I could join you." She had this enchanting habit of lowering her lids when she spoke. Not coquettishly, more a combination of unjustifiable shyness and electrifying mystery.

"Jack Harrington." He didn't extend his hand. He knew it was trembling. All he could do was stare at her foolishly, entranced and unable to still the ferocious thudding of his heart.

"Jillian Ballard," she murmured, sitting down across from him.

He automatically asked if people called her Jill, and then felt like a complete jackass. Jackass and Jill. Great, really great!

"No," she said with a sultry laugh. "But I wouldn't mind if you did. It's kind of funny . . . Jack and Jill."

He laughed with her. He wanted to do everything with her.

That was when he got a good look at her eyes for the first time. What eyes. What extraordinary eyes. He had never in his entire life seen a person with two distinctly different-colored eyes. But hadn't he known on sight that Jill was thoroughly unique. Her left eye was a warm cocoa brown, while the other, quite remarkably, was blue. And not merely your run-of-the-mill blue. The most vivid indigo blue he'd ever seen.

They hardly spoke during dinner. Jack was tongue-tied—realizing she was so close that he could reach out and stroke her arm. And Jill appeared incredibly self-contained and impressively comfortable with the silence between them. She made no attempt at the usual questions vacationing strangers invariably ask one another. None of the "where are you from," "what do you do for a living," "where'd you go to school," "what's your astrological sign." No. No questions at all. She told him she liked the callaloo.

"I think I'll try the conch tomorrow," she added.

He'd had the conch the night before and hadn't cared for it at all.

"I'd love to try it, too," he told her. The hell with his taste buds. "How about trying it together?" he added, his heart pounding, his palms literally sweaty with the anxious thought that she might turn him down. He hummed with joy when she didn't.

The prospect of a second dinner with Jill left Jack restless with anticipation all night. The next morning, despite a lack of sleep, he again took stock of himself in the bathroom mirror and he decided he looked none the worse for wear. Perhaps even a bit more roguishly rugged. He even winked at his reflection and spoke to himself out loud. He was quite far-gone by this time. "You devilish buccaneer, you," he drawled, reddening with embarrassment at the thought of ever being overheard. Then he slipped on his bathing trunks and headed down to the beach.

Jill

Jill hated to fly, and so, on the trip down to Tobago, she tried to still her anxieties with a couple of Bloody Marys. She didn't like to drink very much. She chose the Bloody Marys because she didn't mind tomato juice and the drink seemed appropriately "brunchish". Two brunchish Bloody Marys later, she was feeling dizzy and queasy and still edgy as could be as the plane hit one air pocket after another.

As if the turbulent flight itself, made all the worse by her inebriated state, wasn't enough, just before landing she had to make a quick trip to the lavatory to put in her contact lenses. She'd bought them for the trip, and since she'd hoped to sleep during the flight, which she didn't, she hadn't bothered to put them in yet.

The lenses had been a sort of impulse purchase. Back in Philly, she'd gone into the optician's to buy a new pair of prescription glasses, but she was almost presold on the contacts by the optician's assistant, who confided that her own absolutely extraordinary violet-blue eyes were, in fact, tinted contact lenses. While Jill's eyes were a reasonably pleasant milk chocolate shade of brown, she'd always secretly wished she had blue eyes.

The clever saleswoman nailed down the sale when she claimed, or rather, exclaimed, that with Jill's shade of auburn hair, the change to blue eyes would make her a total knockout. Especially, she'd added, if Jill uncoiled her French knot and tried wearing her hair loose.

After she ordered a pair of indigo blue lenses to match the saleswoman's, Jill stopped at the resort department of Lord & Taylor and splurged on a few sexy sundresses and even some flimsy undergarments, feeling very wanton and very excited at the same time. In her workaday life, she strictly dressed for success. Tailored business suits—grays, blues, a couple of pinstripes—starched cotton shirts, sensible pumps. Well, maybe she was thinking she'd be dressing for a different type of success on vacation. She'd managed to keep it a deep dark secret, but in her heart of hearts she was a dyed-in-the-wool romantic. When she decided on a tropical island vacation, she had visions of a daring romantic escapade, a brief bittersweet love affair.

She had big plans. Well, big dreams, anyway. A gal can dream, can't she? Especially one with flowing auburn hair and dynamite blue eyes. She knew she was getting carried away, which only convinced her all the more how much she needed a vacation. She hadn't taken one in two years and never before to a tropical island. It felt decadent. It felt terrific.

So here she was, standing in the miniature lavatory, looking at her indigo-blue lenses shimmering in their case. She had some second thoughts, but she'd deliberately left her old glasses home, knowing herself well enough to guess she'd lose her nerve otherwise. In the midst of her wavering resolve, she reminded herself that

the optician's assistant had sworn she'd be a knockout
with them. They were comfortable enough during her
practice sessions, and she did like having blue eyes.
She'd already undone her French knot, her hair falling
in loose abandon, as they say, around her shoulders.
Not bad, she had to admit. Then again, without the
lenses in, she couldn't exactly get a very good look at
herself. She put the right lens in first. A vivid blue eye
looked back at her from the mirror. She smiled seductively at her reflection. Maybe not a shattering knockout, but a definite improvement.

She balanced her other blue lense on the tip of her
index finger and was about to delicately maneuver it
into her left eye, when the plane hit a big air pocket and
suddenly lurched. The lens dropped to the floor and she
dropped to her knees in the cramped space trying to
find it. After a minute of being battered about by a
whole series of air pockets, she realized her fear of
crashing was zooming out of control as was her
mounting queasiness. She sat back gasping, saw the
flashing warning sign to return to her seat and rushed
to obey, giving up her search for the errant lens.

The plane descended to a jolting, screeching landing. In her panic, Jill completely forgot about the missing lens. When the plane rolled to the terminal and
came to a safe stop, her fear subsided, but the ill effects
of the Bloody Marys hung on.

It was nearly 6:00 p.m. when she cleared the terminal. She hadn't been able to get down much of the in-
flight lunch, and she figured she needed to put some
food in her stomach quick. At the Hotel Caribe Reef,
she dropped her suitcases in her room, dashed in and

out of the shower, slipped into one of her sexy island sundress numbers and headed to the patio restaurant for dinner.

The instant she stepped through the French doors out onto that patio, her eyes were drawn to a dark-haired man having dinner at one of the tables. He exuded the salty, wicked aura of a seafaring pirate. He certainly had a way with women. The blonde standing by him as he ate looked like she'd like to devour him.

Jill was taken aback when he looked her way. No "looked" was an understatement. He was *ogling* her. Before Jill averted her eyes she gave him a quick side-long glance that she hoped came across as enigmatic. Then she quickened her pace to catch up to the maître d', who was leading her to her table. Right next to her pirate.

She picked up the menu, pretending to study it, all the while feeling his riveting gaze on her. Finally she looked back at him. He smiled. A whammy of a smile. Errol Flynn, in his best pirate films, hadn't done better. She could feel her heart skip at least several beats.

She smiled back with a smile she hoped conveyed shameless confidence, and yet, held a hint of modesty. She had never tried a smile like that before, so she was really winging it. But then, winging it was what this island vacation was all about. She'd indulged herself with optimistic romantic fantasies, and here she was, forget the fantasies, twenty minutes on a tropical island and this remarkably good-looking, sexy man was staring at her as though his eyes were having the feast of a lifetime. No other man had ever looked at her that way.

She went back to a pretend read of the menu, keeping a watch from the corner of her eye on her handsome pirate and the tall, blond vixen. The exchanged a few words, and then, to her delight, the blonde took off in something of a huff. Jill didn't think her pirate even noticed. He was still looking at her. She was still looking at the menu. Truly looking at it now, only to find herself straining to make out the selections. To her horror, she realized she was still wearing only one contact lens—one indigo-blue contact lens. She prayed for her attentive pirate to look away for a moment so she could slip it out. What in the world would this dashing adventurer make of a woman with one blue eye and one brown eye? The thought filled her with dread. She tried to draw the menu up higher to cover her face, but he was leaning over toward her.

"You should try the callaloo. It's made with local seafood. Very tasty," he said.

She kept her gaze downcast and managed a smile she was sure looked dumb. "Thanks for the suggestion," she muttered, her voice unusually low, which always happened when she was nervous.

When the waitress came over a minute later, she ordered the callaloo. Jill wasn't ordinarily so daring when it came to sampling new food, but she thought it might please him. She wanted to please him. To be perfectly frank, she wasn't only thinking of food.

And she must have pleased him with her order, because the next thing she knew he was asking her to join him at his table. He said, "Since we're both alone…"—not "dining alone"—so that meant, like her, he was also by himself in this tropical paradise.

The only reason she hesitated at all about joining him was because of her eye dilemma. But dusk was falling, she rationalized. She could keep her gaze lowered.... Maybe he wouldn't notice that she was this strange lady with one brown eye and one blue eye. To hell with it. She'd have to risk discovery. There was no way on earth she was going to turn that pirate down.

Her mind went racing on. Holding hands, kissing, making love. There she was, thinking about safe sex and she hadn't even reached his table yet. Actually, prior to that point in her life, Jill's life had revolved around her career, and her thoughts about sex, safe or otherwise, didn't really crop up that much. She didn't date very often. And she worked for one of those stodgy companies that entirely forbade mixing business and pleasure. Not to worry. The men at the company were definitely not the stuff of romantic fantasies.

She set down her menu and joined her handsome pirate at his table.

"Jack Harrington," he said. He didn't stretch out his hand to shake hers, which was a relief. Her palms were sweaty with anticipation.

"Jillian Ballard."

"Do people call you Jill?"

She laughed. Even her folks didn't call her Jill. "No, she said, laughing again as she thought about the old Mother Goose rhyme. "But I wouldn't mind if you did. It's kind of funny...Jack and Jill." He laughed. He had the sexiest laugh any man had a right to have. They'd shared their first joke together. She was ready for a whole comedy routine if he suggested it.

Jill tried to maintain her lowered gaze, but she wasn't entirely successful. To her considerable relief, he never said one word about her peculiar eyes. In fact, he was very quiet during dinner. She was thrilled that he wasn't plying her with questions. She had no desire to admit to her mundane life beyond the tropics. She made up her mind to be evasive if he did ask her anything about herself. Maybe he'd think she was alluringly mysterious—a woman with a secret past. She intentionally didn't ask him anything personal, either. It was her way of preventing his throwing the same questions back at her. And maybe she didn't want to learn too much—maybe he was a womanizer, a rogue, a philanderer with a wife and five kiddies at home.

Their silence continued as her empty dinner plate was removed from the table. "I liked the callaloo," she said, lying. Oh, it wasn't indigestible, but it wasn't something she'd ever in her right mind order again. On the other hand, she hadn't been in her right mind since setting eyes on Jack, and if he suggested eating it again she probably would. To be on the safe side, she added, "I think I'll try the conch tomorrow." Conch. She had no actual idea what conch was, nor was she particularly keen to find out, but she figured a man who ate callaloo probably ate conch and she was hoping against hope he'd like to share his joy of eating conch with her.

"I'd love to try it, too. How about trying it together?"

Be still, my eager heart, she thought. "Great," she said. Now she felt compelled to get out of there before she ruined anything. She begged off a rum punch—she was feeling punch drunk as it was—mentioning how light-headed and exhausted she was. Which was the truth. They made plans for the next evening and she excused herself to return to her room.

Jill's first act after locking her door was to go to the bathroom sink and pop out the blue contact lens. Life for the remainder of her holiday was going to be a bit blurry, but she was already so infatuated with her pirate she wouldn't have been able to see straight even with her matched set of indigo-blue contact lenses. So, she'd have to skip the pile of books she'd brought with her. Jack Harrington promised to make for far more colorful reading.

The next morning she ate her complimentary continental breakfast on her private patio—mango, croissant with tropical fruit jam, fresh brewed coffee—put on the skimpy black bikini she'd bought at the resort department at L & T, then went down to the hotel beach for a morning swim.

Okay, what she really wanted wasn't a swim but to bump into Jack on the beach. If she could have seen better she'd have tracked him down, stalked him, followed him all the way to heaven and back. The idea of waiting until dinnertime to be with him felt honestly torturous.

And then, in a sea of blurry male bodies on the beach—lousy eyesight and all—she found him. It must have been her inner radar overachieving.

He was leaning against the counter of one of the thatched gazebo bars a good twenty feet from where she was sitting on her beach towel. She had a wild and crazy fantasy at that moment that she could open her heart and pour it into his. Then they'd be two hearts

beating as one. She had never in her life had such a bla-
tantly hokey thought, but by that time she was so entranced with Jack, hokey didn't trouble her in the least.

While she was having her fantasy, Jack's inner radar
must have kicked into gear, because moments after
she'd detected him, his head turned in her direction and
his eyes zeroed in on her eyes. Her two chocolate-brown
eyes. Well, maybe two indigo-blue eyes would have
been better, but from the telepathic messages Jack was
airwaving in her direction she couldn't believe that the
color of her eyes was going to stand in the way of true
love.

2

JACK KNEW AFTER that very first encounter with Jill that if he valued any speck of his independence he'd take off for the nearest emergency exit. He didn't. They spent that second day on the beach together, ate conch that night for dinner—the conch didn't even taste bad—and walked along the shore in the moonlight. It was a slow, lovers'-type walk—holding hands, their fingers laced together.

"When do you go back home?" she asked. It was one of the few questions she did ask.

Jack couldn't bear to tell her he only had three days left on Tobago. Anyway, he didn't actually start his new job for another week. He'd planned to give himself a few days in his new studio apartment to get settled.

"How long are you staying?" he asked her.

She laughed. He could listen to her laugh forever. "Six more days."

He smiled. "Me, too," he said, praying fervently he could arrange the extension with the hotel. But if he had to pitch a tent and camp out on the beach he'd have stayed.

She squeezed his hand tighter. They stopped walking. She looked up at him with two big brown eyes; she'd told him about the "blue" eye over dinner and they'd laughed together. He told her he loved her eyes just the color they were. Which was the truth.

Her nearness, the way she looked up at him, made Jack feel he was inhaling moon glow. She was wearing a berry shade of lipstick. Suddenly, he was wild about berries. He longed to taste those berry lips, to devour them.

It was crazy, but he was scared to kiss her. Not that Jack was a bad kisser. He'd had a few intimate relationships in his day. And he never got any poor performance reports. But Jill was different. He was madly in love with her. He felt like love was flooding into him so fast, so furiously, he might burst. He didn't know how to play it. He didn't want to rush her, risk her pulling back. He was afraid he'd scare her off. He was afraid he'd lose her.

But the way those chocolate-brown eyes of hers were looking at him, like maybe he really was a rogue pirate . . .

"I want to kiss you," he said, unable to contain the wish. Did a rogue pirate announce his intentions first?

"I want you to," she said, her voice even huskier than usual.

When his lips touched hers he felt a surge of electric excitement. He heard bells. He had his eyes closed and he was seeing stars. The way she slid her body up to his made him feel that was exactly where she belonged.

Her lips were soft, warm, *berry* delicious. Her tropical scent swirled around his brain like an aphrodisiac. He wasn't scared anymore. He was greedy. Their kiss grew wilder, hotter, Jack's hands sliding across her ivory shoulders, then down her back. The warmth of her skin seeped right through her thin black silky mini-dress to his palms.

"I can't keep my hands off you," he admitted, his lips against her hair.

"I'm glad," she whispered, her lips finding their way back to his. He kissed her deeply, sliding his tongue across her teeth, her tongue, the heated recesses of her mouth. She was sweeter, more intoxicating, than all the berries in the universe.

JILL'S LEGS WERE so wobbly as she and Jack made their way back to the hotel from the beach that she stumbled a few times. Suddenly, just before they got to the steps of the grand veranda that circled the hotel, Jack lifted her in his strong arms. He carried her through the lobby, into the elevator, up to his room on the seventh floor. Every eye in the place had to have been staring at them, but she and Jack only had eyes for each other. A volcano could have erupted, hot lava flowing into every corner of the hotel, and Jill wouldn't have noticed. She doubted Jack would have, either. They were both absorbed in one single-minded goal.

When they finally got to his room, Jack didn't turn on the light. He didn't say a word. Neither did Jill. They came together in the dark, their arms circling each other, kissing, their bodies pressing, the tropical night air heavy with their mutual need, their mutual desire.

He stripped off her dress and the only undergarment she was wearing, a pair of black lace bikini panties. Jill was about to make passionate love with a practical stranger and she didn't even have a single doubt about the rightness of it. Before she'd met Jack she'd believed she could only allow her impulses to be expressed in fantasy. But this was reality. Jack was real. Without hesitation, she undressed him, thrilling to the taut, firm feel of his body. She boldly glided her lips across his chest. She could feel his muscles quiver. She'd never felt a man's muscles quiver before. She wasn't completely inexperienced, there'd been a few significant men—a couple—in her life, but no one so responsive. And until Jack, she had never trembled with anticipation, She had never felt passion shoot through her veins; she had never heard her own breath quicken. . . .

Jack could feel his control slipping as Jill's lips started to trail down his body. He started murmuring all sorts of things—how much he wanted her, how much he needed her . . . how much he loved her. It wasn't just bedroom talk. He meant every word. And he wanted Jill to know that. He cupped her chin and drew her face up to his.

"I love you," he murmured, then kissed her with more tenderness than heated passion, wanting her to know, before they made love, that they were doing just that, making love, not merely having sex.

"I love you, too. I've never loved anyone before and I'm never going to love anyone else," she said with an ardor that touched him so deeply, tears welled in his eyes.

Jill was afraid she would scare him off. She'd never spoken so openly about her feelings before. As soon as the words poured out she worried that she'd said too much, sounded too adolescent, too inexperienced. Okay, Jack had said he loved her. Okay, so she'd believed him. But did that mean he wanted her binding her heart and soul to his for life? Jill was terrified that her swashbuckler would panic over the intensity of her feelings for him and back off. Or even worse, make love to her, and then sail the next boat out of Tobago. Suddenly she didn't want a brief romantic interlude. She didn't want the bitter part of the bittersweet affair. She didn't want an affair. She wanted more. She wanted it all.

Jack was embarrassed about his tears. He didn't want Jill to think he was some kind of emotional boob. He was about to make love to the woman of his dreams. He was Robinson Crusoe. Strong, reckless, adventurous, daring. Would Robinson Crusoe have started to blubber if the woman he wanted more than life itself told him she would be his one and only love? Not on your life. So he pressed his face into her hair....

There was such a smoldering intensity about the way Jack carried her over to the bed, burying his lips in her hair as he stretched out over her, his sure hands gliding over her body like she was a delicate bud about to flower and he was the master horticulturalist. His lips joined the tender exploration and Jill went wild with arousal. With what suppressed feelings had she been living with until that moment? Jill followed his lead with a boldness that was entirely new to her. Their lips met again, and she wanted that kiss to touch his soul. Jack's lovemaking took on greater urgency. He was discovering all her secret places. She let out a sharp gasp of pleasure and Jack paused for a moment. She threw her legs around him, holding him fast, afraid he would stop what he was doing, afraid that these wondrous sensations inside of her would end.

His whole body throbbed as he felt Jill's hips begin to move under him. A moist sheen covered her whole body. He had never seen a more exquisite vision—Venus and a glistening tropical island princess all rolled into one. He was beside himself with ecstasy as she cried out her need and desire. He grabbed for the small silver packet he had in the drawer of his beside table.

Finally, when Jill thought she would go out of her mind with wanting him, he filled her, his warm breath falling heavily on her neck. He whispered wonderful love words in her ear, urging her on, telling her what a perfect fit they were, how this was fated to be, again how much he loved her. She only half heard him, so many new and stunning feelings were overwhelming her as they picked up the tempo of their rhythm. Her whole body tingled and then throbbed with a mounting intensity. It was like she was about to descend on the world's biggest roller coaster, an escalating, exhilarating ride to revelation, rapture, orgasm. And when it happened, her heart and soul rejoiced along with her body because it was such a complete act, love and passion combined.

"I love you," he whispered as they lay quietly entwined in each other's arms. "I'll never love anyone but you."

His words thrilled her more than all the words of love he'd said before. It was an affirmation of her own feelings, the feelings she'd risked admitting to him earlier. They had made love, and he wasn't going to hop the next plane out of Tobago. He was going to fall asleep in her arms, and they were going to make love again in the morning. They were going to have six glorious days and nights of making love. And when the six days were over...

Jill really did know nothing about him. Where would he be going on the seventh day? How old was he? Was he married? The fear that he might have that wife and kiddies back home suddenly seemed desperately important. She decided she needed to know some of the vital statistics, anyway. She started with the most important question.

He grinned and answered readily. "I'm single. Never even came close to being engaged. I did go steady with a girl back in high school." His grin turned into a surprisingly boyish smile. "I've never been serious about any woman before," he said with an altogether appealing shyness that snuck through his rugged rakish exterior. Jill didn't tell him how appealing that shyness in him was to her, figuring it was not the thing such an accomplished pirate lover would want to hear.

"I'm single, too," she told him. "I'm twenty-eight, I grew up in a small town in Wisconsin. I'm an only child. I'm allergic to lima beans. And you're far and away the very best thing that has ever happened to me in my life."

He drew her closer to him and laughed softly. He told her he was thirty-four—she'd guessed thirty-five, only a year off, he'd grown up in a suburb of Chicago, he was an only child, and she was the very best thing that had ever happened to him in his life.

And then they discovered that they both lived in Philly. They agreed fate had brought them together, although, in truth, Jill for one had never put much stake in fate until Tobago.

Jack couldn't believe it. Jill lived in Philly. Would their paths ever have crossed if fate hadn't brought them together on Tobago? Not likely. Philadelphia was a big city.

He drew her tight against him, reveling in the heat of her. The very thought that he might never have met her devastated him. He sensed that Jill was feeling the same way. Their bodies moved together again. He sensed that they were both propelled by a new urgency they didn't quite understand. It was as if the very thought that this might not have ever happened but for the hands of fate, made them both want to prove that they were worthy of fate's generous gift.

Afterward, Jack could barely resist the urge to ask her right there and then to marry him. Oh, he knew that was crazy. Who asks a woman to marry him after knowing her little more than twenty-four hours? Only he knew, with absolute certainty, twenty-four hours, twenty-four days, twenty-four months, twenty-four years, he'd feel exactly what he was feeling at that moment. He knew that he wanted Jill to be his wife, that he wanted to spend his whole life with her, that he wanted to love, honor and cherish her till death did them part. Jack and Jill, forever . . .

If Jack had asked her, right then and there, to marry him, Jill's answer would have been a ringing yes. She knew that was crazy, but still, she wouldn't even have hesitated. She was beyond reason, but she had her reasons, nonetheless. She felt she knew everything about Jack she needed to know. She knew he was perfect. She knew his vital statistics. And what's more important, she knew he was warm, tender, romantic, passionate.

Hands down, or more to the point, hands on, she knew he was the most exciting lover any woman could ever dream of. The list of attributes went on forever. Jack was honest and open. He injected life into her. He made her find herself, her true self. Until Jack came along she was only going through life mechanically, without really feeling.... If she'd called to tell her folks that night that she'd just met a man she was willing to marry, they would have said, "You're crazy. It must be sunstroke." Jill wouldn't have argued. They would have probably been right. She did feel a little crazy. But it wasn't sunstroke. It was love.

On Jack's fourth anniversary with Jill—their fourth dinner together—the waitress told them that there was the possibility of a hurricane hitting the island in a couple of days, depending on its course. There were precautions the guests at the hotel should take....

Jack took the most imminent precaution. Over their moonlit creole dinner, he asked Jill to marry him.

IT WAS AN INCREDIBLY romantic proposal. He dropped to his knees in front of her. He grasped hold of her hands—unfortunately one of them was still holding a fork full of creole shrimp which went flying and landed on the front of his white slacks—and he said, "We have to live for the moment, and now that you've come into my life, every moment counts. Marry me, Jill. Marry me here on Tobago. Marry me tomorrow. That way, if the hurricane does come, if this whole island gets swept into the sea, we'll be forever bound together."

The last part of his proposal was admittedly a bit morbid and melodramatic, but Jill didn't for a moment think a hurricane anymore than an erupting volcano would wipe them out. She believed their love made them invincible.

A simple "Yes, I'll marry you, Jack" was all she answered.

She'd barely gotten the words out when he was leaping up, his hands tucking underneath her arms, lifting her to her feet. And right there in the middle of the Hotel Caribe Reef patio restaurant, filled to capacity, he let out a loud whoop of joy and then his mouth met hers.

Every diner and staff person out on that patio burst into enthusiastic applause. Jack held her close and they laughed and she cried. And though Jill couldn't swear to it—her sight was too blurry—she thought Jack cried, too.

Jill was incandescent with joy. Through her tears and laughter, she whispered to him. "I'm the luckiest woman in the world." And she was convinced, as long as she had Jack, she'd be forever blessed with good luck.

And I'm the luckiest man," Jack whispered back, too thrilled and excited to even care if Jill saw the tears spilling from his eyes.

He took her hands and kissed each of her fingers. He told her that first thing tomorrow he'd buy her a wedding ring and talk to the minister of the quaint little white stucco church on Englishman's Bay about performing the ceremony. Then he announced the news formally to all and sundry on the patio, inviting every one of them to the wedding.

THE NEXT MORNING, while Jack went to arrange things at the church, Jill rushed into town to hunt down a wedding dress. Nothing elaborate, just something white, soft and flowing. She found the perfect dress in Scarborough, Tobago's capital city. At a little outdoor market, no less. It was white eyelet cotton with a scooped neck and ruffled skirt that fell softly to mid-calf, and it came with a multicolored, handwoven cumberbund that closed with tiny gold buttons in the shape of hearts.

When Jill told the vendor she was going to wear it for her wedding that afternoon, the woman congratulated her in her soft exotic-sounding Creole patois. Then, when Jill handed her the money—a steal at twice the price—the woman insisted upon throwing in a beautiful white lace scarf to wear as a kind of veil. Her wedding present. Overwhelmed by the display of generosity, Jill gave her a big hug and invited her to the wedding. The woman's dark-skinned face lit up with excitement, and she asked if she could bring along some family and friends. Sure, Jill told her. Bring as many as you like.

Tobago is a tiny island, and not exactly a shopper's paradise. Jack wanted to get Jill a really special ring. Not only was the selection meager or way out of his price range, nothing much caught his eye. He was beginning to lose hope when he happened upon, not a shop exactly, but a small cottage near Pigeon Point. The entry was beneath a bower of brilliant red bougainvillea. In one of the front windows was a small hand-painted sign reading James Ivory, Artisan and Jeweler.

The cottage door opened as Jack started up the path to see if Mr. Ivory made rings. A very tall, very bulky man with golden skin, much of which was exposed as he wore only a pair of white swimming trunks, greeted him with a pleasant nod.

"You're looking for James, right, man?" He spoke with a heavy Caribbean accent.

"Yes. Well, actually, I was looking for a ring. A wedding ring."

He grinned, revealing two gold front teeth. "You've come to the right place, man," he said cheerfully.

Jack wasn't convinced. The husky Mr. Ivory with his large hands did not look the sort to make the kind of ring Jack envisioned adorning the delicate finger of his true love. He must have taken a step back because Mr. James Ivory stepped forward and threw a hefty arm around his shoulder and gave him an exuberant congratulatory shake.

"So, you're getting married. Fantastic, man. Fantastic. Come in. Come in. We have to toast."

James Ivory left Jack no chance to argue. Maintaining a firm grip on his shoulder, the artisan ushered Jack into the main room of the stone cottage. It was pleasantly cool inside and charmingly decorated with locally made wicker chairs and chaises, the cushions and pillows done in batik and tie-dye prints. The stone floor was softened by natural sisal mats. Bamboo shades covered the windows, blocking out the hot morning sun, but letting in enough light to give the space a cheery, homey look.

Jack found the whole feel of the room surprisingly feminine. Then he met Mrs. James Ivory, who came out of a back room. She was as petite as James was huge. Indeed, she was a contrast to her husband in very way. Fair-haired, green-eyed, she had a delicate bone structure and all of her gestures were light and graceful.

James introduced Jack to his wife, Laura, and immediately followed up by telling her Jack had come for a wedding ring.

She was as delighted by the news as her husband. "Why, how nice. When is the wedding?" she asked in a thick British accent.

"This afternoon, actually. At St. John's Church on Englishman's Bay."

Laura and James shared a smile. "That's where we got married. Almost five years ago," James explained.

"James and I met and fell in love here on Tobago."

"Laura was a travel agent who was island-hopping for her company. You know, sampling the hotels and restaurants."

Laura picked up. "I fell in love with Tobago the moment I saw it. I wanted to bring something back to London that would always remind me of the island." They both laughed before Laura went on. "I came out here to Pigeon Point and met James on the beach."

"I was working on a coral necklace and Laura came over to admire it."

"*Admire* it? I positively went gaga over it. Exquisite coral stones threaded with gold. It was extraordinary." She smiled. She had a winning smile.

"She went gaga, too, when I told her the price," James said and chuckled. "I was teasing her, you see.

Because I planned to give it to her. It was meant for her, you see? I knew the moment I set eyes on her."

"You mean...you fell in love with her...right there...right then?" Jack asked, taken aback. Had some voodoo kingpin cast a magic spell over exotic Tobago?

"Ah," James replied, his eyes twinkling, "so you think you are the only ones, you and your future bride, to fall in love at first sight? You think, perhaps, you invented it, man?"

Jack laughed. "How did you know it was love at first sight for me and Jill?"

"It is written all over your face, man," James said with a broad grin.

A minute later, they all toasted Jack's upcoming marriage with a refreshing white wine. Then James showed Jack a simple but elegant ring he'd only just finished making, a one-of-a-kind, woven-gold wedding band studded with shimmering black coral. Exactly right for Jill and, to top it off, well within Jack's budget, although he had the distinct feeling that James had specially lowered the price. By way of thanking him, Jack invited James and Laura to the wedding.

James gave Jack a hearty slap on the back. "Well, friend, you will be needing a best man, anyway, right?"

"Yes," Jack said, delighted to have this jovial, warm-hearted fellow who understood all about love at first sight, stand up with him.

WHEN JILL GOT BACK to the hotel, there was a note from Jack waiting for her at the desk.

The pastor of St. John's will arrange everything with the town magistrate, and the ceremony is set for four this afternoon, my love. See you at lunch. All my love.

Jack.

Jill checked her watch. It was a little past noon. She went into the dining room where the maître d', a dapper middle-aged man with gray hair combed straight back, greeted her like an old friend. She explained that Jack would be along shortly, and he showed her to a choice table, moments later returning with a very fine bottle of champagne.

"Why, thank you. That's very nice."

He made a big fuss of setting the champagne in a silver ice bucket, carefully, meticulously, wrapping a white linen cloth around the neck of the bottle. He continued to hang about, adjusting the table setting, smiling brightly if a bit bashfully.

When Jill responded with a questioning smile, he hemmed and hawed a bit, then asked if Jack's open invitation to the wedding had been seriously meant.

"Why, of course."

"That's good. Some of the staff were talking. Well, it's not every day two guests meet and well . . ."

"We'd be thrilled to have people from the hotel come to the wedding. Neither Jack nor I know a soul on the island, and the thought of there being no one in the church . . ."

"Then none of your families are coming?" he said, sounding quite concerned.

"Oh, no. I haven't...we haven't told any of them yet. It's all been...rather whirlwind."

The maître d' swirled the champagne bottle in the ice bucket. "Then you'll have no one to...give you away?"

Jill smiled and shook her head. She hadn't actually thought of being given away. She hadn't actually thought of there being a wedding ceremony in the formal sense. Actually she'd been too busy and too ecstatic to do much in the way of thinking about anything.

The maître d', who hurriedly introduced himself as Henry Theodore Porter, bowed formally and asked if he might then have the honor of giving the bride away.

Jill was dumbfounded but quite touched. He pointed out, and she readily agreed, that he had played a hand in bringing her and Jack together since he'd seated them at adjoining tables that first night. Jill told him she'd be honored to have him give her away.

JACK THOUGHT JILL LOOKED breathtaking in her white dress—the most beautiful bride in the world. Courtesy of the hotel, they arrived at the church on Englishman's Bay in an open hansom cab. They were both speechless as they entered the church. It was filled to capacity. Overflowing. Standing room only. They recognized a number of staff and guests from the hotel, and then there was James, fitted out now in crisp white trousers and a ruffled orange silk shirt, and Laura, prettily dressed in a brightly colored print skirt and pale yellow blouse that set off her blond hair. Waiting just inside the door beside James and Laura was the maître d', whom Jack and Jill now both fondly called Henry. Henry was decked out to the nines in a formal tux, crisp white shirt, and black bow tie.

The lady from the marketplace who'd sold Jill her wedding dress was sitting in one of the back pews with a half-dozen children and a large group of friends, some of whom Jill recognized as other vendors at the market. The rest of the wedding guests looked to be local islanders who'd gotten the word that a good party was in the offing. They added a warm touch of local color and a wondrous air of festivity and joy to the occasion.

Jack and Jill thought it the most wonderful and miraculous wedding anyone could have ever dreamed up. Way beyond their expectations.

Six days ago they hadn't met a single one of these people, or each other, for that matter, and now practically every person either of them had met on the island was there to witness their marriage.

A couple of members of the Hotel Caribe Reef's steel band began playing the wedding march with a delightful reggae twist. The guests swayed a bit to the rhythmic island beat.

Jill felt radiant, almost electric. She was delirious with joy as she slipped her arm through Henry's arm, and they began walking together down the aisle past all the cheery well-wishers lining the pews. All eyes were on her, and she was loving every moment.

Jack was spellbound as he stood beside his best man, James, at the altar, and watched his luminous Jill float down the aisle toward him. He wondered if any man had a right to be this happy.

Jill's eyes spilled over with tears of happiness as she finally linked hands with Jack. She was sure she'd found paradise on earth.

As Jack slipped the exquisite handwrought gold-and-black-coral ring on her finger and the pastor pronounced them man and wife, they felt finally whole and complete.

Jack and Jill forever . . .

PART II

JACK FELL DOWN AND BROKE HIS CROWN
AND JILL CAME TUMBLING AFTER....

3

"ARE YOU SURE you want another Bloody Mary, Jill?"

Jill gave her new husband a wilted look. "Believe me, Jack, I'm sure."

Jack motioned to the stewardess. "Another Bloody Mary for my wife." He hesitated. "And I'll have another bourbon and soda."

Jill cast Jack a wayward glance. "Is that three or four?"

"I'm not sure," he admitted.

"Do you...usually drink...a lot?" she asked nervously.

"No, not usually. Do you?"

"I hate to drink." She managed a weak smile. "It's just...I hate to fly more."

"Do you? Hate to fly, I mean?"

"Yes. Do you?"

"Not...usually." There was an open magazine on Jack's lap, but without his glasses he couldn't focus on the words. Or maybe it was nerves. Jack was certainly nervous. His shirt was plastered to his skin with sweat.

"Jill, we need to...talk." His voice held a hint of desperation. At some point soon he had to come clean. For one week, swept away by passion and romance, he'd thrown caution to the winds and donned the style and personality of a rugged seafaring buccaneer oozing with an animal magnetism that no woman could resist. What would Jill think when she found out that his real-life persona was as far removed from a buccaneer as Philadelphia was from Tobago?

Jill cast her new husband an anxious look. "Talk?"

"I mean . . . we should . . . get better acquainted."

For all her nervousness, Jill had to laugh. "I guess we did put the cart before the horse."

Jack placed a tender kiss on her cheek. "I'm not sorry," he whispered.

She trembled at his touch. He was so wonderful, so sexy. Her heart pounded with the excitement of just being near him. "Neither am I," she whispered in response.

He smoothed back her untamed auburn hair. "My wild, exotic island princess," he murmured.

Jill's throat went dry and she was suffused with guilt. "We really . . . should talk, Jack."

Before they could work their way into a frank conversation pitting harsh reality against tropical fantasies, however, a perky brunette stewardess came along with their drinks.

"Hey, congratulations. One of the passengers just told me you two are newlyweds." The stewardess gave them both a disbelieving look. "Is it really true that you had a whirlwind courtship down in Tobago and got married after knowing each other for just a week?"

"Six days . . . actually," Jill admitted. Six days. It usually took her longer than that to decide whether to buy black pumps or navy. She'd agonized for a month over what to get her mother for her birthday. She was still trying to decide whether to buy a new bedroom set and it had been a year. She had never made important decisions impulsively. Well . . . almost never.

Jill snuck a glance at Jack. He was so handsome, so sexy, so virile. He really did remind her of a swash-buckling pirate. And just what was her pirate husband going to make out of the real-life Jillian Ballard? She wished he'd stop calling her his "wild, exotic island princess". Back in Philly she was about as wild and exotic as the Liberty Bell.

"Gosh, that's so romantic," the stewardess was drawling. "I once fell in love with a guy down on Jamaica. He was an absolute doll. We hit it off the minute we met. Spent two glorious weeks together. We were going to write each other after our vacation, and we had all kinds of plans to get together. I really thought he was the one."

"What happened?" Jill asked.

The stewardess laughed dryly. "I got one letter. A postcard, actually. And then, a few months later, I bumped into him in San Francisco. He looked absolutely gorgeous." She skipped a beat. "If you happen to go for guys in dresses."

"Dresses?" Jill sputtered, quickly taking a large swallow of her Bloody Mary.

The stewardess gave a world-weary shrug. "I'll say one thing for Al. He had great taste. I would have killed for the stunning Perry Ellis number he was wearing."

"But you said you knew him for two whole weeks," Jill muttered, her stomach doing a disquieting flip-flop.

"When we were together in Jamaica, I never saw him in anything but bathing trunks, jeans and T-shirts. He was an absolute hunk." She leaned a little closer. "But

I wouldn't be surprised if, while I was in the bathroom showering, he was modeling all of my tropical island sundresses in my hotel bedroom," she whispered conspiratorially. "Really, the things you find out about a person."

Jack and Jill stared at the insensitive stewardess with grim looks, but she gave the newlyweds a cheerfully oblivious smile and went off to attend to her duties.

Jill gulped down the rest of her Bloody Mary.

"Hey, take it easy," Jack said softly. He reached for Jill's hand. It was cold and clammy. "I swear, I never tried on a single one of your dresses while you were showering," he said with a teasing smile.

Jill grinned, albeit a little crookedly. Those Bloody Marys really were going to her head. "How about my nighties?"

"Never. Scout's honor." He pressed the palm of her hand to his lips. "But I do love those nighties on you. And I love taking them off you even more."

"Jack . . ."

"Mmmm?"

"Do you think what we did was crazy?"

He nibbled one of her fingertips. "A little."

"Do you do . . . crazy things a lot?"

"No, not too often," he admitted, feeling a sinking sensation in the pit of his stomach. "Jill . . ."

Jill let her head fall onto his shoulder. "It really was romantic. Incredibly romantic." She let out a long sigh.

Jack pressed his lips to her honeysuckle-scented hair, but he could feel the sweat zigzagging down his back. "Nothing like this has ever happened to me before, Jill. Do you know what I mean?"

"Mmmmm."

He let his head sink back against the seat and closed his eyes. "It was incredibly romantic."

"Mmmmm."

"I love you, Jill."

"I love you, Jack."

"Maybe . . . we should . . . talk."

She lifted her head and her eyes met his, a soft smile on her lips. "Later. We'll talk later. We've got a whole lifetime to get better acquainted." She kissed him tenderly. For just a short while longer, she'd be his wild, exotic island princess.

ON THEIR FIRST MORNING back from Tobago, Jack woke up at the crack of dawn and left Jill's apartment—now their apartment—and rushed across town to his studio so that he could dress for work. When he was done, he stopped at the superintendent's to say he'd be moving out that afternoon and would have to sublet. Luckily the superintendent knew someone who was looking for a sublet and he didn't think there'd be any problem. That was one dilemma solved. Unfortunately Jack doubted his other problems would have such easy and satisfying solutions.

Jill was consumed with plenty of worries of her own that morning. Firstly, she had not yet confided in her new husband that his wild, exotic island princess was, in real life, a straitlaced, conservative investment officer for the August Foundation, a stodgy philanthropic organization that provided private research grants for social and scientific projects. While she loved her job and it gave her prestige, status and a very good salary, it was about as unglamorous as slinging hash.

Also causing her a fair amount of concern was the pressing problem of how she was going to tell Howard Wendell August, the pompous, self-righteous president of the venerable August Foundation, that one of his most reliable, down-to-earth and responsible employees had come back from a one-week vacation with a husband in tow. August was bound to be shocked and consider her action highly suspect and irresponsible.

As Jill began dressing for work she mentally reviewed her schedule for her first day back. For starters, she had a meeting with August and the new head of the physical science grant evaluation team. She'd have to hurry if she wanted time to prepare. Shoving her personal worries to a back burner, she swallowed down a quick cup of coffee and rushed downstairs to catch a cab.

The August Foundation was housed in an 1860s stone manor house in the exclusive Chestnut Hill section of the city. As befit the foundation's prestige and venerable reputation, great care had been given to creating an environment that would reflect impeccable but restrained good taste. The reception area was paneled in a burl wood imported back in the 1860s from England. The oak parquet floor was covered by an oversized oriental rug. Well-placed around the room were small groupings of brown leather armchairs and mahogany coffee tables. Oil paintings of English hunt scenes decorated the walls. The offices themselves all echoed the same simplicity of color and design. Any changes in decor had to have the approval of the president himself. No one at the foundation put in such requests.

Jill crossed the reception area and paused just outside August's outer office. She adjusted her black-rimmed glasses, made sure no loose hairs had escaped her French knot, and smoothed down imaginary wrinkles from her gray wool skirt, making sure she was in ship-shape order before making an appearance in front of her boss. Even though she'd had to rush getting dressed that morning, she'd taken care to wear an outfit that exuded a primly neat and efficient aura—gray flannel suit, soft white blouse buttoned up to the neck and adorned with a plain string of pearls, sturdy black leather pumps. She opened the door, her body stiffening and her eyes lowered, as if she were entering some sacred place.

Cynthia Adams, August's attractive secretary from South Carolina, gave a brief nod of greeting as Jill entered. She was a new addition to the foundation. August's last secretary, Milly Reeves, a sweet-natured woman with blue-gray hair, had retired a month ago. Everyone had been surprised that August had hired such a pretty young southern belle with flaming red hair, although in August's defense, for all her attractiveness Cynthia was certainly reserved, curt, efficient, dedicated—the perfect August Foundation secretary.

"Did you have a pleasant vacation, Jillian?" Cynthia asked politely.

"Pleasant?" Jill had to smile. "Yes, it was very pleasant."

"Mr. August left these notes for you. He wants you to look them over and he'll buzz for you in a few minutes." She handed the papers across to Jill with crisp, no-nonsense efficiency.

Jill glanced down at the printout. "Is the new guy here already?"

"Yes, Mr. August is talking with him now." Cynthia went back to her computer workstation.

Five minutes later, August buzzed for Jill.

As she opened the door to her boss's inner sanctum, Jill smelled the familiar aroma of old leather mingled with a lemony scent of polish. Usually a comforting scent, today it put her on edge. Then again, it didn't take much to put her on edge today.

"Ah, here she is now." Howard Wendell August gushed. "The pride of the August Foundation, my exceptional chief investment officer." He was a small, dapper man in his early sixties with short-clipped gray hair and a pinched expression. He spoke with a slightly affected English accent, even though he'd been born and bred in Philadelphia.

As her boss made the introductions, Jill paid little attention, just snatching a quick glance at the scientist, a man with slicked-back dark hair, horn-rimmed glasses, an unstylish navy blue suit and unfashionable black oxfords. No doubt quite brilliant, but not exactly prepossessing.

Jack rose as the young chief investment officer took a seat, and absently pushing his glasses back up the bridge of his nose, he gave her a distracted glance. No doubt very competent and highly efficient, but not exactly a heart-stopper.

He automatically extended a hand in greeting. "It's a pleasure to meet you."

Jill responded in kind, but as she took hold of the scientist's hand, she felt a lurching sensation in her chest.

All of Jill's glorious tan drained from her face, her features a study in incredulity. No, no, no, she told herself, it isn't possible. It just isn't possible that this bland and utterly unglamorous-looking scientist really was her swashbuckling pirate.

Taken aback by the woman's tight, unyielding grip on his hand, Jack gave her a curious look. And then he looked a little closer, curiosity giving way to shock.

A tense silence hung in the air as they stared at each other, their hands remaining clasped together in a rigid, viselike grip.

"Jack . . . ?" she said, almost sotto voice.

"Jill . . . ?" The papers in his free hand fell to the floor.

"Yes, yes, first names are fine," August said with an officious little smile. "But do call her Jillian, Jack. Our Jillian's not one for nicknames." He gave a little chuckle. "You don't want to get off on the wrong foot with our chief investment officer here, Harrington. Jillian's the very backbone of our foundation."

Jack Harrington didn't hear a word his new boss was saying. He was in a state of shock. Surely this was some sort of bizarre nightmare and any minute the alarm clock would go off and he'd wake up in bed beside his wild, exotic island princess.

But the alarm did not go off. All that happened was that Howard Wendell August cleared his throat, his expression one of dismay at the sight of this rather strained and awkward greeting between his two employees. He expected all members of his staff to behave toward each other with cordial propriety, nothing more, but nothing less.

"You might want to pick up those papers, Jack," August said with forced joviality.

"Papers?" Jack shot him a dazed look.

Jill glanced down. "The papers you dropped," she whispered hoarsely. She found it hard to move her lips. They felt paralyzed.

It took great effort for Jack to pry his eyes off her, to shake himself free of the shock. It took even greater effort to make sense of what she was saying.

Finally, her words penetrating, Jack glanced down. "Oh, right . . . papers." He dropped immediately to his knees to retrieve them, but unfortunately Jack forgot he was still clasping Jill's hand. He nearly tugged her out of her seat.

"Here . . . let me . . . help you," she said in a halting voice.

"I . . . can manage." Jack's voice was barely audible.

Jill watched in stunned silence as he retrieved the papers. She couldn't have been more astonished if she'd bumped into her swashbuckling pirate on the street and found him wearing a dress!

As August launched into a welcoming speech, Jill's shock slowly gave way to anger. How could Jack have deceived her like that, pretending to be a suave, worldly rogue?

During the whole half hour that Howard Wendell August droned on about his goals and expectations and expansion plans for the foundation, Jack remained incredulous, his eyes constantly drifting over to Jill. A wild, exotic island princess, indeed! How could she have deceived him like that?

"HOW COULD YOU . . . ?"

"What do you mean, how could I? How could *you* . . . ?"

"Will you keep your voice down, Jack. We can't talk here," Jill said anxiously, casting a nervous glance around her office as if the walls literally had ears. "August doesn't condone his staff people getting into arguments."

"How about arguments between husband and . . . ?"

She clamped her hand over his mouth before he could finish. "Jack, didn't you read the August Foundation Rules of Conduct sheet? Fraternization between colleagues is grounds for termination. Marriage is . . . even worse."

"We obviously didn't know we were colleagues when we got married," he countered, pushing his glasses back up on the bridge of his nose.

"Shhh. Please, Jack. Don't even say the word. Oh, this is awful. This is just awful." Weak with confusion and the aftereffects of shock, she sank into her chair, pulled off her glasses and gave him a wan look.

Without the glasses, with a few strands of her hair loosened from her French knot, and with the heightened color in her cheeks, Jill now bore a clearer resemblance to Jack's wild exotic island princess. He came over and knelt beside her.

"It's sort of funny," he said softly.

A weak smile flickered on and off Jill's lips. "Your hair looks dreadful greased back."

He grinned. "I didn't want to risk a haircut. I figured I could degrease it before I got home, stow the glasses, toss my jacket Frank Sinatra-style over one shoulder, give you one of my lean, sexy looks, and you'd never guess that in real life I was a rather shy, reserved scientist that women have a tendency to see through. Down in Tobago . . . well, I guess I loosened up a little." His grin broadened. "A lot."

"I loosened up, too. A lot," Jill admitted with a sheepish smile.

For a moment, as Jack reached out to enfold her in his arms, Jill forgot that she was about to embrace her colleague husband right around the corner from Howard Wendell August's office. A few quick raps on the door brought her sharply back to reality. With a little gasp she vigorously pushed Jack away.

He lost his balance and landed flat on his butt just as Jill's office door opened, and August's austere redheaded secretary popped her head in the door.

"Oh," Cynthia gasped. Nothing at the Reed Secretarial School had prepared her for something like this. "Is anything wrong, Mr. Harrington? Are you ill?"

Jill shot Jack a beseeching look, terrified that he'd blurt out the truth. And she had good reason to be scared, as Jack *was* on the verge of that explanation. But Jill had made her point about the Rules of Conduct and he thought the better of it.

This is what he came up with instead. "I was just showing . . . Miss Ballard . . . Jillian . . . a good . . . back exercise. We discovered we both have . . . lower backache . . . on occasion." He pressed the palm of his hand to the bottom of his spine as he rose from the floor. Then with a quick, nervous smile, he stretched. "There. Much better."

Cynthia, her lips pursed, stepped into the office.

Jill felt like crawling right under her desk. Lower backache? She could just see August's shrewd secretary buying that one.

The nostrils of Cynthia's aquiline nose flared as she narrowed her eyes on Jack.

Jill held her breath waiting for the ax to fall.

"Where is it you feel that ache, Mr. Harrington?" Cynthia asked. "Right on the base of the spine?"

Jack and Jill exchanged quick glances. "Uh . . . yes. Right on the base of the spine," Jack said slowly, returning his hand to the imaginary ache on his back.

Jill immediately followed suit. "Yes, we both have it in the same spot," she muttered inanely.

"Well, isn't that peculiar," Cynthia remarked with what Jill took to be clear suspicion.

"Well, I don't think—" Jill started to say, only to be cut off by August's secretary.

"You must show me that exercise, Mr. Harrington," Cynthia said with earnest sincerity. "I have the exact same problem in that exact same spot. If there's some sort of exercise that can relieve the pressure when those muscles down there tighten up, I'd be ever so grateful."

Jill gave Jack a wry smile. "Yes, do show Cynthia that exercise, Mr. Harrington."

Jack smoothed back his greased hair and then readjusted his glasses. He wondered if he looked as uncomfortable as he felt. "Well, it's not exactly a . . . cure-all, you understand. And every back is different. Sometimes an exercise is good for one person and . . . not so good for another." He offered up a decidedly goofy smile. "I'm afraid I tend to be overzealous at times. Perhaps you . . . both . . . should check with your doctors about . . . the right exercises."

Cynthia looked truly disappointed. "Well . . ."

"Did you want something else, Cynthia?" Jill quickly asked.

"Oh . . . yes. The three o'clock meeting with the Burton group has been postponed until Wednesday. Same time. They did send over those papers you wanted, though. Of course, Mr. August wanted to look over them first. He says if you have any questions or problems with the update, to stop by his office and he'll be happy to discuss any troubling issues." Cynthia placed the thin manila folder on Jill's desk.

"Thanks. I'll go over these and get back to Mr. August if I have any new concerns. And I'll change the appointment to Wednesday in my book."

Cynthia nodded and walked toward the door. Halfway out, she turned round to Jack. "You might want to brush off . . . your pants . . . Mr. Harrington. Mr. August takes great pride in his staff being tidy and well-groomed. If you do feel the need to do back exercises at work with any frequency, perhaps you'd like to bring in an exercise mat."

Jack worked hard at keeping at straight face. "Yes, perhaps you're right, Cynthia. That makes good sense."

She smiled curtly and exited.

Jack was grinning broadly when he turned back to Jill.

Jill, however, looked like her features had been carved in granite. "You've got to leave, Jack."

He toned the grin down to a smile. "You're right. First day and all. I have to get settled."

"No," she said sharply. "I didn't mean leave my office. I meant leave, period. We can't both work here, Jack."

"Why not?" he said breezily, still quite pleased with his back problem story.

"Why not? Why not?"

"Quiet, darling. August frowns on conflicts between his tidy, well-groomed employees." He brushed off the seat of his pants and pivoted round for Jill's inspection. "Better?"

Jill flinched. "Jack, I'm serious. We can't both stay working here. And I certainly have seniority. So, it's only fair that you go."

He turned back round to face her. "Go? No, I can't do that, Jill. Do you have any idea how long I've been angling for this job? The August Foundation has national acclaim. Heading one of its departments is my ticket to success. It's a once-in-a-lifetime opportunity. I know some people who would kill for a job like this."

"I know some people who could kill, too," Jill said tightly.

"Be reasonable, Jill."

She was reasonable. She was always reasonable. That just showed how much he knew her. "Listen to me, Jack," she began in a low whisper. "I've been at the foundation for seven years. I started at the bottom and

I clawed my way to the top ranks. And if you think it's easy clawing when you have to wear white gloves, you're sadly mistaken. I've sacrificed plenty to get where I am. And I'm not about to walk off meekly into the sunset and let you waltz in. If I play my cards right, I just might work my way into a vice presidency."

The sudden appearance on Jack's face of his roguish Tobago smile was completely out of context with the rest of his buttoned-down appearance. "Well, that's great, Jill. Sexy and ambitious. I like that in a wife."

Jill grit her teeth. "I'm not sexy, Jack. You just…think I am. I'm not any of the things you think…or thought." She hesitated. "I really wasn't myself down in Tobago. Obviously. Maybe it was the tropical air, or too much sun, or the aqua sea, or the palm trees…or…voodoo magic." She dropped her head into the cradle of her arms on her desk. "What have we done, Jack?"

"We've fallen madly in love," he said softly.

Slowly she lifted her head, made a show of putting her glasses back on and smoothing back the unruly strands of hair that had broken free of her French knot. As Cynthia said, August Foundation employees were expected to be tidy and well-groomed. "No, Jack. We didn't fall in love." Her lower lip quivered despite all her effort to be stalwart. "A swashbuckling pirate and a died-in-the-wool career woman who foolishly pretended to be a wild, wanton island princess fell in love. It was a fairy tale, Jack."

"Fairy tales have happy endings, Jill."

"Does that mean you will hand in your resignation?" she asked hopefully.

Jill knew the honeymoon was over when Jack smiled benignly and said, "Now what kind of a happy ending would that be?"

"Jack, if you think I'll relent and toss in the towel, you've got another thing coming. I'm not quitting, and if you don't quit, we'll both end up getting fired. And I'm not one of those starry-eyed romantics who's willing to sacrifice her career for true love."

"Jill, Jill, you don't have to quit. I don't have to quit. And we're not going to get fired. Trust me, my wild, wanton island princess. Haven't you ever heard the saying, love conquers all?"

4

JILL MANAGED TO AVOID Jack for the rest of that day, but she remained shaken and distraught. All of her colleagues, expecting to find her relaxed and well-rested after such an exotic island vacation, were at a loss to explain her edgy manner. And Jill was certainly not about to explain it to them.

After work, Jill hurriedly left the foundation so that she wouldn't bump into Jack. Meanwhile, Jack went off to rent a small van so that he could move his still-unpacked cartons from his studio apartment to Jill's place. Fortunately no furniture was involved as he had rented the studio furnished.

The process of moving out took close to an hour, but it went smoothly enough—what with the superintendent coming through with a sublet and all, but there was nothing smooth about the move into Jill's apartment.

"Jack, maybe...you shouldn't have...moved out...of your place...so fast."

Jack dropped the heavy carton of books he was lugging onto the hallway floor. "Married people usually live together," he said softly. "Besides, the superintendent already sublet my studio." He smiled at her. "Come on, help me with the rest of the cartons and we'll sit down and...get better acquainted."

"There are a lot of problems here, Jack," she persisted.

He picked up the carton again. "Like where are we going to stow all my stuff? I'm afraid I'm making a bit of a clutter. But we'll sort it all out in time. So, where should I put the books for now?"

Jill knew that Jack knew that those were not the kind of problems she meant. But she supposed she would have to make space for him in any event. "Oh...I guess the spare bedroom...for now."

He crossed the living room with the carton of books. Jill, still dressed in her business blouse and skirt, picked up one of the lighter cartons, an open box stuffed with odds and ends, that Jack had carried in with the books. She commented on a gold-painted trophy lying on the top of the box.

"For chess." He grinned. "I'm afraid I was never big on sports. How about you?"

Jill shrugged. "I once won a ribbon for swimming."

"Swimming. That's great. So you're a swimmer."

"I won it when I was seven."

He stopped at the doorway to the spare room and looked back at Jill. "By the way, we were so busy last night...settling in—" He smiled, remembering "—I never did tell you how nice your place is. Not just the apartment. I mean the way you've decorated it." He gave a sweeping look around the small but cosy living room with its warm peach-painted walls, gray carpeting and colorful print sofa and matching loveseat grouped in front of a working fireplace.

"I bought everything from the last tenant," Jill muttered. "I'm afraid I'm not really...into decorating."

"I'm not into decorating myself, but I'm pretty good with my hands."

Jill felt her cheeks warm. She could certainly vouch for that.

Jack grinned, having accurately read her mind and feeling a rush of pleasure. "Small carpentry projects. With the addition of all my books, we might want to build another couple of bookcases. What do you say?"

Jill didn't know what to say. She just stared at this unprepossessing man in his drab navy business suit, studious black-rimmed glasses and unbecoming hairstyle, feeling at a total loss for words. She kept thinking of what the stewardess had said on the flight home. *The things you find out about a person.* Still, now that some of the shock had worn off, she had to admit a drab business suit was a long sight better than a cute little Perry Ellis number.

It took about a half hour for the two of them to finish unloading the van and transporting everything upstairs in the elevator to her fifth-floor apartment. The last item was a large garment bag. Without asking, Jack carried it into Jill's bedroom, Jill followed on his heels. She was slowly dissolving into misery over all of the unresolved issues pressing in on her, and she made up her mind not to put off her concerns another moment or Jack would be wiping her up off the floor. She decided to tackle the most imminent problem first. Then they'd go on from there.

"Jack, you've got to face it. We absolutely can't both work at the foundation," she said with a frantic edge to her voice as she followed him right over to her closet.

Jack opened the closet door. "Not much room here."

She gave him a distracted look. "Maybe you should use the closet in the spare bedroom." When she saw the funny look he gave her in response, she added begrudgingly, "Just until we get . . . organized."

"We can tackle that this weekend," he said pleasantly.

Jill noticed an open carton of his socks and underwear on the bed. She picked it up to bring next door.

Jack gave her wry look. "I don't usually hang those items up."

"My dresser's pretty full, too," she muttered. "The one in the spare room is empty."

In the small spare room, now crowded with most of Jack's belongings, he unzipped his garment bag and hung his suit in the closet. Jill set the carton she was carrying in front of the dresser. She thought of stowing away his things for him, but something held her back. It felt too intimate. She realized that was a pretty dumb way to feel, considering all the other intimacies they'd shared. But, she argued with herself, they'd shared those other intimacies under false pretenses. Under the glitter of tropical stars, golden beaches, sapphire bays. Down in Tobago it had all been so magical . . . so unreal. Stark reality held no such glitter.

"What are we doing to do, Jack?"

He took off his suit jacket and hung it up. "I don't know about you, but I'm going to jump into the shower. Care to join me?"

"I don't mean—" She came to an abrupt stop and shot him a nervous look. "What are you doing now?" she asked as he unzipped his trousers.

"I usually get undressed before I shower. Don't you?" His trousers dropped to the floor and he stepped out of them.

"Don't be cute, Jack."

"You liked me being cute in Tobago."

"This isn't Tobago. And we can't have a . . . meaningful discussion with you standing there in your boxer shorts."

He grinned. "I could take them off."

"How can you be so . . . so . . . ?"

"Sexy? Provocative? Roguish?" he teased, offering up his best buccaneer smile.

"So impossible."

"Come on, Jill. You worry too much."

"How do you know how much I worry? We've spent a total of six days together."

"Seven. One whole week. Happy anniversary, darling." He managed a quick kiss on her lips before she backed off.

"Jack, you've got to take this more seriously."

"I take it very seriously," he protested. "For richer, for poorer, in sickness and in health, for better or worse . . ."

Jill sank down on the narrow guest bed. "It doesn't get much worse," she said mournfully, feeling the sting and ache of tears behind her eyes.

Jack went over to her and lightly stroked her face. "Then it can only get better," he whispered, smiling rakishly. Glasses, greased back hair and all, the man was a charmer. There was no doubt about that. Whatever had happened to him in Tobago hadn't worn off. She couldn't say the same for herself. Now that she was back in Philly, she felt depressingly divorced from the carefree woman she'd been in Tobago. She'd taken such pleasure in indulging all her erotic impulses with utter abandon. Now trying to connect with her island princess persona, Jill felt only embarrassment and discomfort.

She turned away from Jack, propping her chin on one hand, elbow pressed into her thigh. "Oh, Jack, my life has always been so predictable. Maybe it was mundane, but who's to say mundane is so bad. Okay, maybe there are no big highs, but there are no big lows, either."

"We had some great highs in Tobago. I'll take that over mundane any day." He removed first his glasses, then hers, setting them side by side on the bed. "When we were in Tobago, you told me you loved those highs."

She grabbed her glasses, returned them to their rightful place and got up from the bed, wishing Jack would put his pants back on. Instead, he was unbuttoning his shirt. She tried to focus her eyes past him, feeling a need to hold on to her new image of him as a nerdy-looking scientist rather than be reminded of that bronzed Adonis who'd swept her completely off her feet only one week ago.

"We've got to settle this problem about the foundation, Jack. You don't know August. He's a paragon of virtue and an absolute stickler for propriety. You've only been at the foundation for a day. You can't imagine how fiercely August holds his staff to his strict code of ethics and prescribed rules of professional etiquette. Once, a couple of years back, he bumped into two of his people coming out of a movie theater arm in arm, and he fired them both the next day. If August finds out we're married, he'll have a fit and we'll both lose our jobs. What sense does that make?"

"He doesn't have to find out," Jack argued, slipping off his shirt.

Frustrated and angry as she was, Jill's eyes couldn't help a quick skidding glance over his broad golden chest. Along with the glance came an alarming and unwanted rush of desire. Once again, she looked past him. "It's not going to work. I'm not a good liar, Jack."

"You're not going to lie," he said with a sly smile as he approached her. "You're just not going to mention that one of the things you happened to do during your one-week holiday in Tobago was get married."

"But don't you see how much simpler and easier it would be if we weren't working together?" she persisted, stepping back, keeping her eyes averted. "It's going to be hard enough to ... adjust to our lives together without making everything immeasurably more complicated and tense. Think of what a strain it will be, seeing each other every day at work, having to pretend we're little more than strangers, when in reality we're climbing out of the same bed every morning."

Jack smiled provocatively. "Think of the spice it will add to our lives, Jill." He put his arm around her and kissed her—a warm, friendly, good-natured kiss tinged with an edge of excitement.

Jill tried her level best not to be aroused, but she could feel herself slowly, irrevocably, losing the battle. She refused, however, to admit defeat.

"It's not spice. It's crazy. It's ... schizophrenic," she argued.

Jack's eyes lit up. "Hey, think about your everyday superhero for a minute."

Jill gave Jack a narrow look. Maybe he was schizophrenic. "Superhero?"

"Sure," he said blithely. "Doesn't your typical superhero spend his off-hours looking like an ordinary, mild-mannered, Milquetoast sort of guy? Superman, Clark Kent, that sort. And no one who sees this ordinary Joe ever cottons on to his dual identity. That's the whole point...."

"Jack, Jack. You're talking comic books and I'm talking real life. Real life, with real unemployment lines. Which we'll both end up being on if one of us doesn't write that letter of resignation." She gave him a tight, narrow look. "And you already know which of us I think should write that letter."

Ignoring her fury, Jack placed both hands lightly on her shoulders. "You know what's happening, don't you?"

She tried to hold on to her indignation for protection, and not to be distracted by his melting glance. "What's happening?"

"We're having our first marital squabble."

"Oh," she muttered as Jack's hands slid down her back and he drew her closer. She really wished he wasn't standing there bare-chested, in his boxer shorts. It was extremely distracting.

"That means we get our first chance to kiss and make up," he murmured against her ear.

"I don't want to make up," she protested, although even she could hear the lack of authority in her protest.

"The kiss comes first, anyway."

"No, Jack. Not until we settle this," she argued, struggling in vain to get out of his grasp.

"Give it some time, Jill. Like you said, we have a lot of adjusting to do. We're not going to do it all over night. Why not concentrate on those areas that we already have some practice in? Do you realize that this is the longest we've ever gone without . . ."

"Let me go, Jack. This . . . this whole thing . . . isn't going to work. We're just . . . deluding ourselves. It was all a delusion. Don't you see that?"

He refused to loosen his hold on her despite her protest, and her vehemence was fading fast as she found herself instinctively responding to the pressure of his body against hers. What madness had she gotten herself into? She decided it was all the fault of that violet-eyed saleswoman who'd sold her those contact lenses just before her trip to Tobago. If she'd just bought a new pair of sensible glasses and not gotten so carried away trying to be someone she wasn't, she wouldn't be in this impossible predicament.

"Jack, we've got to be sensible about all this," she pleaded.

He took firm hold of her shoulders, his expression intense. "Listen, Jill, I'm thirty-four years old and I've spent a lifetime being sensible. Sensible, level-headed, rational, restrained, always thinking and rethinking every move I made. As for women . . . well, to say I wasn't exactly a ladies' man before I met you is to put it mildly. I was always awkward around women. I was the sort of guy who, if a woman handed me a cigarette to light for her, would stick the wrong end in my mouth and the filter tip would flare up in my face. If I took a date out for dinner, I'd invariably spill some of the meal either on her or me, or topple over a glass of wine. It would always be red wine, of course. As for any prior wild, exotic sexual encounters, they never . . . came my way. Oh, there was the occasional intimate moment, but to be absolutely honest—" he paused, an endearing smile lighting his whole face "—and I do want to be absolutely honest with you from now on—those moments were few and far between and not exactly the stuff of which dreams are made."

His eyes danced as they raked her face. "Something wonderful happened to both of us in Tobago. We came alive. We didn't simply let our hair down and throw caution to the winds. Don't you see, Jill? We discovered something in ourselves and each other that's exciting, exhilarating and wonderful. You, Jill Ballard Harrington, may be reserved, plain Lois Lane by day, but by night, my darling, you are truly the stuff of which dreams are made."

"Oh, Jack, you're crazy. Or else you must still be punch drunk from those tropical island drinks. I've never been anyone's *dream*. You don't even know me."

"Maybe you don't really know yourself, Jill."

"But I do. That's my problem, Jack." She thumped her chest. "This is the real me. I'm uptight, straitlaced, conventional, irritatingly cautious. Oh, I might have had fantasies about living a wild, exciting life, and, yes, I even acted them out with you for a brief time, but in my real life I'm about as daring and abandoned as a spinster librarian or a maiden aunt."

She gave him a shy but earnest look. "Okay, you want to talk about relationships with the opposite sex — the last man I dated told me I reminded him of his mother. If I'd accepted another date with him, he'd probably have brought along his socks for me to darn. Then, a while back, I was seeing a stockbroker. When we did finally go to bed together, he brought his *Wall Street Journal* along so that he could read it afterward. Aloud." She let out a sharp laugh. "For all I know, he read some of it while we were making love. I kept my eyes closed."

"You didn't keep your eyes closed when *we* made love," Jack said seductively. "And I never read the *Wall Street Journal* before or after sex." He drew her into his arms and began carving an erotic path of kisses up her neck. "Doesn't that count for anything?"

"You're sidetracking the issue." She let out a little gasp as he pressed her closer and slipped his cool, strong hands under her shirt. "What...are you doing?" Jack's hands were inching up her bare back. She felt as if her jumble of emotions was poised mid-juggle right over her head.

He placed a moist kiss on each of her eyelids as his hands traveled around to her breasts. "Sidetracking the issue," he murmured.

"We can't get anywhere this way, Jack."

"Wanna bet?"

"Meek, mild-mannered, ordinary Joe, huh?"

He laughed huskily. "That's just my front, sweetheart," he said with a superhero leer, undoing the clasp of her bra. "Care to step into the shower with me now?"

She let out a ragged sigh of defeat, admitting to herself that defeat had never felt so wonderful. "Don't you mean the phone booth, Superhero?"

THEY HELD EACH OTHER in a soapy, slippery embrace. Then, tilting Jill's back slightly, Jack gently kissed the soft rounded curve of one breast than the other, watching with delight as her rosy nipples grew erect.

"You taste so good," he whispered.

"It's the soap."

"On you, it tastes great."

They kissed with the shower roaring down on them like a waterfall.

His soapy hands caressed her buttocks.

She laughed, ticklish now.

He grew hard between her soapy thighs.

Her laughter faded, her breath coming in quick, ragged puffs.

The world outside the steamy shower vanished. They weren't in Philly. They weren't even in Tobago. They were in a world of their own making, a world in which they were the only inhabitants. Fantasy, reality, it was all one, as Jill became one with Jack.

WHILE NOTHING AT ALL had been solved about their work situation, as Jill puttered around the kitchen looking for something to throw together for dinner, she felt inexplicably light-headed and optimistic. Well, there was an explanation. Jack had been right. A dizzying interlude of lavish, lustful lovemaking in a steamy hot shower had somehow managed to make all of her problems seem amazingly inconsequential.

Jack popped into the kitchen, with a bath towel wrapped around his waist. A glistening sheen of moisture from the shower still clung to his bronzed body. His dark, wavy hair, towel-dried and no longer laden with grease, was once again the wild, tousled mane of a rogue pirate.

Jill turned to him, the way a plant turns to the sun. "I'm afraid it will have to be scrambled eggs. There isn't much else. We'll have to go shopping...."

"Shopping together. Doesn't that sound nice," he said, watching her beat the eggs. In her bathrobe, with her auburn hair once again cascading down over her shoulders, her face shimmering with a dazzling blend of suntan and afterglow, she displayed not a hint of spinster librarian or maiden aunt.

"I guess we can go...after work...tomorrow." She shut her eyes. Maybe it was insane, but maybe they could pull off working together. Scientist by day. Superhero by night. Would the real Jack Harrington please stand up?

He crossed the room and held her close, tight, never wanting to let her go. The towel slipped from his waist. It wasn't scrambled eggs he wanted.

"You're...insatiable," she whispered with a mix of alarm and delight.

"I have never made love to a woman in the kitchen," he murmured, nibbling her ear as his hands moved to the tie of her robe.

"Jack, this is positively decadent. This is...Philadelphia."

"I know." He slipped the robe over her shoulders. Underneath, she was naked. "What would the meek, mild-mannered, ordinary souls of the world think?"

Her robe slithered to the floor and she snuggled into the welcome warmth of his body. Jill said, "They'd think we were a wild and crazy pair."

"Wild and crazy. Go figure," he whispered with a teasing smile.

She gasped when he drew her down to the cool tile floor. The contrast of the chilly floor and Jack's heated body covering her was almost unbearably pleasurable.

With a little laugh, Jack removed the eggbeater still clasped in Jill's fingers. "That's too kinky, even for a superhero," he joked.

Just as the joking ended, the doorbell rang. Jill's eyes shot up to Jack's with anxious alarm. "Who's that?"

He grinned. "Fuller Brush man? Bible salesman?" He nuzzled his lips into her neck. "Let's ignore whoever it is and maybe they'll go away."

There was a second series of rings, this time more insistent.

"I better go get it," Jill said with breathless reluctance. With a weighty sigh, she rose to her feet.

"You'd better put your robe back on, my luscious vixen, or that bible salesman will think he's died and gone to heaven."

Jill laughed and reached for her robe. "Don't move. I'll be right back."

Still smiling as she got to the front door despite another spurt of rings, Jill fit the chain into its slot and opened the door to tell whoever was selling that she wasn't buying.

Her smile dropped from her face with a thud. "Oh, no," Jill gasped, shutting the door fast and leaning limply against it.

More rings. Loud knocks. An anxious, muffled voice.

"Jillian? Jillian? What's wrong? Please . . . open the door. Are you okay? Should I run for help?"

Jill shut her eyes. This was all she needed. Eleanor Windsor had to be the last person in the world she wanted to see just now.

Jack popped out of the kitchen. Stark naked. Jill shot him a look of alarm, and pressed a finger to her lips.

"Just a minute, Eleanor. Be. . .right there," Jill called out. Her breath came in shallow pants.

More knocks. "I'm going to get the superintendent, Jillian."

"No, no, no," Jill cried out. "Nothing's wrong. It's just . . . I'm not dressed. Hold on." As she called out to the persistent woman on the other side of the door, she raced across the room to Jack.

"Quick," she whispered to him in a panic. "Get dressed, hide, get out of here. If Eleanor sees you here . . ."

"Who's this Eleanor?"

"Eleanor Windsor. One of my assistants at the foundation. Don't just stand there. Put that eggbeater down."

"Jillian? Jillian?" Eleanor's shouts grew increasingly urgent.

"What does she want?" Jack asked.

"I don't know what she wants. But she's the biggest busybody at the foundation. Oh, God, what are we going to do?"

Jack gave her a quick kiss. "Open the door and find out what she wants. I'll duck into the spare bedroom and you can call me out when the coast is clear."

Jill's head bobbed up and down. "Right. Right, I'll find out what she wants and you'll stay in the spare room until she leaves."

"I won't budge."

"Jillian? Is someone in there with you? Jillian? Jillian, if you don't open the door this minute, I'm getting the . . ."

Jill raced breathlessly back to the door and threw it open. "Oh, hi, Eleanor. What a surprise!"

"Jillian, what in heaven's name has gotten into you?"

"Into me?" Jill felt her face heat up. "Why . . . nothing?"

"Do you have company?"

"Company?"

"I thought I heard a man's voice."

"The radio."

Eleanor Windsor, with her see-all green eyes, pink cheeks and light brown hair in a bun on top of her head, twitched her pert nose. Jill thought Eleanor's nose was her best feature, although men would have selected another part of the small but shapely young woman's anatomy. Eleanor was, as they say, well-endowed.

"Jillian, you forgot, didn't you? You completely forgot."

"Forgot?" Jill echoed weakly.

"I thought when you saw I wasn't at work today you'd remember why."

"Why?"

"The painters came today, Jillian," Eleanor said, exasperated.

"The painters." Jill gave her assistant a blank look.

"Yes, the painters." Eleanor's expression turned to concern. "Jillian, are you all right? Is there someone...?"

And then it struck Jill like a steamroller hitting her in the gut, knocking the wind out of her. "Oh, the painters," she gasped. "You're getting your apartment painted."

Eleanor reached down and picked up the suitcase beside her that Jill had failed to notice. "Well, are you going to let me in?"

Jill's heart was racing. "Well...I..."

"You did promise I could stay with you for a week while the painters were in my apartment. You know how allergic I am to fresh paint."

Eleanor brushed past Jill and headed straight across the living room. "I'll just stick my suitcase in the spare room and hang up a few things. Have you eaten yet? I thought maybe we could call in for pizza. They're showing *Gone with the Wind* on TV tonight. Uncut. All five hours. Won't that be fun?"

"No," Jill said sharply.

Eleanor was within five feet of the door to the spare room. She turned and gave Jill a hurt look. "You don't think it would be fun?"

"No. I mean...you can't...use the spare room."

Eleanor's forehead furrowed. "Why in heaven's name not?"

"Because . . . because . . ."

Before she could think of even a lame excuse, the door to the spare room opened. Jack, wearing a pair of hip-hugging jeans and nothing else, came sauntering out. "Because I'm using the spare room at the moment." He gave the astonished visitor one of his infamous buccaneer smiles.

Eleanor Windsor was not a woman to be easily rattled. but so astonished was she at the sight of the tall, handsome, half-naked stranger popping out of Jill's spare room, that her mouth fell open and her lips actually quivered.

5

INCREDULITY AND HORROR fused on Jill's face. She bore
the expression of a patient who'd just learned her death
was imminent. Terror, shock, fury—she had all the
requisite reactions, none of which altered the hard, cold
reality.

As for Eleanor, she was staring at Jack with the rapt
intensity of a biologist unearthing a new, marvelous
species. Having finally managed to regain a modicum
of self-control, her lips formed into the kind of circle
smokers use for making smoke rings. Instead of a perfect circle of smoke, however, a low, dazed "oh" puffed
out as she stared directly into Jack's bare, bronzed
chest.

Jack wagged a finger at Jill. "Why didn't you tell me
you were expecting a houseguest, babe? I'm surprised
at you. You're usually so efficient and organized." His
voice had suddenly assumed a baffling western twang.

"I...I...forgot," she stammered, thinking that Jack
must truly have gone over the edge. What's more, he
was dragging her over the precipice with him. By tomorrow morning, everyone at the foundation, most
importantly Howard Wendell August, would know the
truth. Did Jack really think he could talk August out of
firing them both on the spot?

Jack could see little sparks of fire in Jill's eyes, but he merely grinned and said, "That trip to Tobago must have been a wallapalooza. I've never seen you so discombobulated. Too many of those spiked tropical fruit punches, is my guess."

Jill started to sway, and it had nothing to do with the aftereffects of alcohol.

Eleanor, managing with obvious difficulty to tear her eyes away from Jack, gave Jill a concerned look. "I hope you didn't pick up some sort of tropical . . . bug down on that island, Jillian."

Jill shot a few invisible daggers at her husband. "Bug?" she mumbled. *Close.*

"I must say, Jillian, you don't look at all well," Eleanor went on, with a concerned expression. "And you're acting rather strangely. Why you haven't even introduced me to your . . . friend."

That's no friend. That's my husband.

Jack saw the mounting distress on Jill's face and jumped right in, grabbing hold of Eleanor's hand and pumping it in a warm, friendly shake. "J.R.," he said with a wide grin. "John Raymond Ballard, actually, but all my friends call me J.R."

Jill stared at him, blinking. J.R.? John Raymond? Jack really was going mad.

"Just like that fellow in *Dallas*," Eleanor murmured, demurely lowering her lids and addressing his bare feet.

"Well, now, I'm nothing like that no-account character, I assure you, Miss . . . ?" He raised a questioning eyebrow.

"Eleanor. Eleanor Windsor," she gushed, hanging on to his hand as if she were pumping for pure gold. "And

I didn't mean to in any way disparage your character, J.R.," she assured him earnestly.

He winked at her, discreetly managing to extract his hand. "No, I'm sure you didn't, Eleanor. I was just pulling your leg. Folks are always teasing me about my nickname. If you'd rather call me John . . ."

"Oh, no," Eleanor said, eyes wide. "J.R. is . . . just . . . perfect." Her cheeks were flushed.

"Or you could call me Jack. That's what Jill and the folks sometimes call me, especially when I irk them."

"What did . . . you . . . say?" Jill stammered.

"I said you, Mom and Dad sometimes call me Jack." He raised his voice a notch and carefully articulated each word slowly, then gave Eleanor a knowing smile. "Swimmer's ear, I bet. If I know Jill, she probably spent too much of her vacation in the water. Jill's a heck of a swimmer. Won a ribbon when she was just seven years old. The whole family was so proud of her. Not to brag or nothin', but I taught her how. To swim, that is. Fast learner. Show her something once and she picked it up like that." He snapped his fingers.

Eleanor beamed. "You're Jillian's brother?"

"Why, Eleanor, who did you think I was?" Jack said with a seductive smile.

"I thought . . . well, I'm not quite sure what I thought," Eleanor gushed, her cheeks again reddening because, of course, she knew exactly what she had thought—that she'd caught her boss cohabitating with a gorgeous hunk. She turned to Jill. "You never mentioned you had a brother, Jillian. Why, I always thought you were an only child," she said accusingly.

So did I, Jill thought ruefully. Okay, Philadelphia was the City of Brotherly Love, but Jack was taking the saying a little too literally for comfort.

Jack put a brotherly arm around his "sister." "Well, I'm not all that surprised Jill hasn't talked me up. Truth is, Jill and I had a little falling out a few years back. She kind of got on me to settle down, take life more seriously, find myself a good wife. She accused me of being rootless and adrift. I'm afraid," he said sheepishly, really getting into character, "unlike my sister who's reliable, wonderfully predictable and as steady as a rock, I've always been sort of spontaneous, impulsive, always throwing caution to the wind."

Jill glared at him but said nothing.

Jack ruffled her hair and then smiled at Eleanor. "You've sort of walked in on a reunion between me and Jill," Jack said, casting Jill a quick, sly wink. "Isn't that right, sis?"

He really was schizophrenic, Jill concluded, having little choice but to nod agreement. *The many faces of Jack Harrington—swashbuckling pirate, meek, mild-mannered scientist, superhero, and now...big brother, J.R. For all she knew, he just might really show up in a dress one of these days. At this point she probably wouldn't even bat an eye.*

"Well, isn't that nice," Eleanor cooed. "I do think it's so important for family to be close. I've got two sisters and I think the world of them both."

"I'm sure you do," Jack said amiably, his eyes coming to rest on Eleanor's suitcase which she'd set down on the floor. "I guess my timing isn't very good. I just arrived last night with everything I own and stowed it

all in the spare room. Jill's letting me stay here with her
until I get settled."

"Oh," Eleanor said, dishing out an eager smile, "so
you're moving here to Philadelphia? For good?"

"That's what I'm thinking."

It wasn't what Jill was thinking, but she had to admit, dear old brother, J.R., had come up with a great
way to get rid of Eleanor. Her assistant couldn't very
well stay with her for the week if her brother was settled in the only spare room.

"I'm really sorry about this, Eleanor," Jill said, her
throat so dry that her voice had a low, raspy quality.
"You see . . . I didn't know . . . J. R. was coming. I was
so . . . excited to see him . . . I just didn't think about . . ."

"Well, of course you didn't, Jillian. I understand
perfectly," Eleanor said.

"Oh, I knew you would, Eleanor. You're just . . . that
kind of person," Jill stammered.

"I don't see any problem, really," Eleanor went on,
her eyes, like twin beams of radar, honing back in on
Jack's big, broad, naked chest.

Jill was taken aback by Eleanor's uncontrollably
lustful leers at Jack. Eleanor Windsor had always pre-
sented herself as a rather priggish, virginal type who
gave the impression she rated chastity over just about
everything but rising quickly up the August Foundation ladder. There was nothing chaste about the hungry way Eleanor was staring at Jack Harrington,
undressing him with her eyes. And even though Jill
continued to be furious at Jack for this new impersonation of his, she did not appreciate the way Eleanor
Windsor was coming on to him. *The cheap little hussy.*

"What did you say, Jillian?"

"Me?" Jill answered, startled. "Nothing. I mean . . . I was just trying to think about where you could . . . go." *And how fast.*

Eleanor smiled seductively at Jack. "I don't see any problem with staying right here," she said blithely, although Jill detected a distinctly stubborn edge to the statement. "I'll just camp out on the couch in the living room."

"Oh, no. You can't," Jill blurted out.

Eleanor was appalled by Jill's lack of hospitality.

"I mean . . . it wouldn't be very . . . comfortable for you. Would it . . . J.R.?" Jill quickly amended.

"Pretty lumpy-looking sofa, if you ask me, Eleanor," Jack said pleasantly. "If I didn't have a mass of junk piled ceiling-high in the spare room, I'd gladly offer . . ."

"I wouldn't dream of it, J.R. Before Jillian got the bed for the spare room, I slept on the couch for a couple of nights while my apartment was being fumigated. It was perfectly comfortable. Remember, Jillian?"

"But Eleanor," Jill said, clutching her robe, "do you really think it would be—" she took Eleanor's arm and turned her away from Jack "—proper?" she finished in a whisper.

Eleanor laughed as she pivoted right back around to face Jack. "Your sister is worried about propriety, J.R., but I see nothing scandalous about this situation. Why, Jillian here can certainly be considered the perfect chaperone. Or is it chaperoness?" She giggled, delighted by her little joke, and clearly more than delighted at the prospect of getting to know Jill's handsome brother a lot better.

For once, Jack couldn't think of a comeback.

"Good," Eleanor said, rubbing her hands together gleefully, "then it's settled. This is going to be fun." She beamed at Jack. "So tell me, J.R., have you ever seen *Gone with the Wind*? I do declare, J.R., you remind me so much of Rhett Butler. You've just got to watch the movie with us."

Jill fumed. *The cheap, pushy little hussy!*

THEY ATE PIZZA and sat in the living room watching *Gone with the Wind*, all of them lined up on the couch, Eleanor maneuvering a position in the middle. Under the best of circumstances, Jack and Jill would probably have enjoyed the florid romance, the grand spectacle, and especially the passion of the film. But this was far from the best circumstance. Indeed, they would both have been hard put to come up with a worse one.

Eleanor, however, was thoroughly enjoying herself. Clutching a wad of tissues, she demurely dabbed away at her eyes. "Oh, J.R.," she sniffed at frequent intervals, "aren't I being silly? I guess I'm a born romantic. So sentimental. I just can't help that I always feel things so deeply." For a moment, here and there, she rested her hand on Jack's thigh, but she never left it there long enough to be crudely indiscreet. Just long enough for Jill to want to commit murder.

Jack felt for Jill, but he also had to admit he took a secret pleasure in Jill's jealousy. He'd been well aware, ever since that momentous meeting in August's office that morning, that Jill was having second thoughts not only about the situation at work, but about their marriage as well. A little well-placed jealousy might help her see just how much she loved him even if there were a few loose ends to iron out. He fully intended to spend the rest of his life with Jill, and they'd have all the time in the world to do whatever ironing out was necessary.

Jill was fuming. She knew perfectly well that Jack was deliberately playing on her jealousy. What's more, he seemed to be thoroughly enjoying this new charade. And what in the world did he intend to do, she wondered, when the morning rolled around and her superhero had to switch back to mild-mannered nerd?

Jack sniffed a little. "I guess I'm the sentimental type, too, Eleanor," he said, extracting a tissue from her hand and blowing his nose quickly.

This time Eleanor's hand not only found its way to Jack's thigh, it lingered for an extra couple of seconds. "Why J.R., I'm moved. Most men I know are so out of touch, or afraid to show their emotions. It's utterly refreshing to meet a man who lets himself show his feelings so openly." She gave Jill, stiffly sitting on the other side of her, a quick smile. "This brother of yours is very special, Jillian. I can't quite picture you two coming from the same family."

Even the obtuse Eleanor could hear the unintended insult in her remark and she flushed scarlet. "Oh, I didn't mean ... I just meant ... you two are just so different ... in temperament and style. Not ... not that you're cold-hearted, Jillian. I mean ... you're just so ... self-contained and ... unflappable. I admire those qualities. I've always said I wish I could be more like you, Jillian. It can be a curse being the sort of person who feels things so deeply."

Jill clasped her hands tight to keep them from springing around Eleanor's neck. They spent the next half-hour in edgy silence.

"So, J.R., what are your plans now that you've decided to settle in Philly?" Eleanor simpered during the film's intermission. "Have you found a job here yet?"

Jack stretched. "No, I'm not feeling any big rush. Thought I'd check things out."

"What is your profession, J.R.?"

Jill raised a brow. "He's sort of a *Jack* of all trades," she muttered.

Eleanor emitted a little squeal. "Why Jillian, that was quite funny."

Jack grinned. "Jill does have an amusing side to her nature, Eleanor. Once she warms up."

"Really?" Eleanor said, surprised. "I guess I've never seen that side. Jillian's generally so serious and intense."

Jill clutched her hands together more tightly. The urge to strangle Eleanor was fast getting out of control. And she wasn't feeling any too kindly to dear brother J.R., either. One more jabbing innuendo from him and she just might throw caution to the wind herself. At the moment it was definitely touch and go.

The intermission had ten more minutes to go. In preparation for Part Two, Eleanor grabbed up a new supply of tissues, this time handing Jack his own wad. Jill rose from the couch.

"Where are you going, sis?"

"I've had enough." Jill deliberately paused before adding. "Of the movie. I'm going to bed."

Jack popped up from the couch. He had no desire to be left alone with the smitten Eleanor.

"Well," he said stretching, "I think I'll turn in as well."

Eleanor's disappointment was palatable. "Oh, you can't desert me now, J.R. I hate crying to the second half of *Gone with the Wind* all by myself," she said plaintively. "Besides, it's only ten-fifteen. I'd have thought you were a late-night person just like me."

"You're a late-night person?" Jack was hoping, once Eleanor dropped off to sleep, he'd be able to sneak out of the spare room and creep into bed with his wife. As long as he made it back to the spare room before dawn, he figured Eleanor, fast asleep on the couch, would be none the wiser.

"I never turn in before one in the morning, J.R."

"Even on workdays?"

"I've always been a person who could operate on very little sleep. Nervous energy." Eleanor gave him a seductive smile.

"Well, surprising as it seems, Eleanor," Jack said with another stretch, "I'm an early-to-bed, early-to-rise kind of guy." He grinned in Jill's direction. "Some habits we learned as kids just don't change, huh, sis?"

"You are so right, Jack," Jill said tightly.

Jack winked at Eleanor. "Uh-oh. See how she called me Jack? That means she still hasn't fully forgiven me yet."

Jill gave Jack a dark glare. "There are some things you just can't rush, *J. R. Ballard*."

"Oh, Jillian, you two have to kiss and make up. Life is too short to waste it on petty disagreements," Eleanor scolded.

"My feelings precisely, Eleanor," Jack said enthusiastically, grabbing hold of Jill before she could make her escape. He pulled her to him for a big bear hug, playfully nuzzling her neck.

"Will you let go of me," Jill ordered through clenched teeth. "Jack, stop it this instant. Jack. J.R. Stop..."

"When we were kids, Eleanor, Jill and I would wrestle like nobody's business," he said, chuckling and maintaining his hold on his squirming *sibling*.

He had her off her feet, and Jill, in anger and desperation, gave him a swift kick in the shin.

"Ouch. I bet you never guessed Jill was such a little vixen, Eleanor," Jack teased, pretending to ignore the pain.

"I never did," Eleanor said, clearly envious of Jill's current captive position.

"Jack, I'm warning you..." Jill hissed.

He hoisted her over his right shoulder, fireman fashion. "Hey, remember how I used to carry you to bed this way when you were little?" He started for Jill's bedroom. "Gee, isn't it fun reliving old times?"

Eleanor giggled. "Jillian, I swear no one at work would believe how you carry on with your big brother."

Jill, her upper torso hanging down over Jack's back, stopped kicking her feet, lifted her head and glared at Eleanor.

"Oh, not that I'd ever say anything about it," Eleanor said hurriedly. "I think it's great that you and J.R. can...fool around so...freely." She waved gaily as Jack opened Jill's bedroom door, stepped inside with her, and closed it shut behind him.

"I will never forgive you for this, Jack." Jill's words came out in a rush as he dropped her onto the bed.

"Shh. Eleanor might hear us."

"You're insane, Jack Har—"

The rest of his last name was swallowed by his brief kiss.

"How could you..." she started again, shoving at his chest.

"Did you have a better idea?" he whispered. "If I hadn't come up with something fast, your buddy Eleanor..."

"She is not my buddy," Jill said emphatically.

"Maybe not, but she is your temporary roommate."

"Yes, your clever little plan certainly backfired. Now what do you intend to do, brother J. R.?"

He grinned. "I don't intend to finish *Gone with the Wind*."

"I'm not talking about tonight...."

"I am. Listen, as soon as Eleanor slips off to dreamland, I'll slip in here and ..."

"Oh, no, you won't. God, that's all I need. Eleanor spreading rumors about me having a love affair with my own brother. Or did you somehow think August would look more kindly on incest than on marriage between employees?" she asked facetiously.

"Well, at least J.R. doesn't work at the foundation," he teased.

"This is not one bit funny, Jack. What happens tomorrow morning? How do you intend to turn back into Jack Harrington without Eleanor noticing?"

"Simple, I'll leave the apartment before Eleanor wakes up, find myself a nearby phone booth, and presto chango, I'll turn myself into Clark Kent."

"I can see it now. Some cop comes strolling by the phone booth in the middle of your presto chango and you blithely exclaim to him all about superheroes and their quick-change requirements," she said sarcastically.

"Okay, maybe a phone booth would be too cramped, anyway. I'll change in a public rest room at one of the office buildings down the street."

"We can't keep this up all week, Jack. You'll have to...take a hotel room...at least until...Eleanor leaves. I'll tell her that we just don't get along and we both agreed it would be best...."

"I think you just want to get me away from Eleanor. I do believe you're jealous, Mrs. Harrington."

"I'm too angry to be jealous."

"Don't be angry, Jill. Eleanor's not my type. And as for a hotel room, what way is that to start off a marriage?" He gave her a teasing smile.

"Aren't you forgetting another minor glitch in your plan? Eleanor is going to see Jack Harrington at the foundation tomorrow. What happens when she discovers that Jack Harrington and J. R. Ballard are one and the same? Then what happens?"

"Nothing happens," he said airily.

"Jack..."

"Nothing happens, because Eleanor won't even give dull, drab, out-of-touch Jack Harrington a second glance. She won't notice me. That is, she won't notice the *me* that's *him*. She'll be all caught up thinking about the me that's your brother. I'll just melt into the woodwork, no more noticeable than some old shoe. The me that's him, that is. As for the me that's your husband . . ."

Jill closed her eyes and shook her head. "I've married a certifiably crazy person."

"I am crazy about you, Jill." Jack stroked her hair from her face, then edged the folds of her robe open. "More as my wife than my sister," he teased, forcing a weak smile from Jill.

Her smile lingering, she started to protest nonetheless. "What's Eleanor going to think about you being in here with me so long? You'd better . . ."

"Are you still angry at me, Jill?" His hands lightly, playfully, cupped her breasts.

"I'm trying," she murmured weakly, letting out an audible gasp of pleasure as his seduction took a more serious turn.

"Jack, Eleanor will hear . . ."

"She can't hear anything over the sound of the TV. Gasp to your heart's content, darling."

"Jack, we can't do this. It's indecent."

Jack's eyes sparkled. "Later then? After Eleanor's asleep?"

Jill sighed. "A part of me knew this was madness right from the moment I laid eyes on you. I mean, what person in her right mind marries somebody she's known for three days?"

"I was ready to marry you that first day. But I thought I shouldn't rush you," he teased.

"Rush? I feel as though I've gotten stuck in a revolving door that just keeps spinning faster and faster."

"We'll work everything out," Jack soothed, cradling her in his arms. "All we have to do is take it one day at a time. Trust me, Jill."

"Trust who?" she asked wanly, going limp in his arms. "Superhero, colleague, brother?"

He grinned. "All three of me."

"Are there any more?" she asked nervously.

There was a light rap on the door. "J. R.?"

Jack and Jill exchanged glances. Then Jill rolled her eyes up to the ceiling.

Jack's grin deepened. "Yes, Eleanor?" he twanged, refusing to release Jill even though she tried to break free.

"The intermission is over. Part Two is starting. Are you sure you don't want to watch the rest of the movie with me, J.R.?"

"Jill and I are just . . . reminiscing about the . . . old days . . . when we were wild and carefree kids." He nibbled on Jill's ear. "We have some catching up to do." His lips made their way to her throat. He could feel her pulse racing.

Jill was having serious difficulty coordinating the demands of her mind with the actions of her hands, which were trailing rebelliously down Jack's back.

Eleanor was still hovering on the other side of the bedroom door. "Oh. Well, you should really let Jillian get some rest, J.R." She emitted another of her little laughs. "You may not know this about your sister, but she does get a bit . . . grouchy . . . when she hasn't had enough sleep. I do have to work with her tomorrow."

"I swear," Jill muttered under her breath. "I am going to murder that woman before the week is out. What am I saying, week? She may not survive the night."

"Temper, temper, sis."

"And don't think your neck is safe either, J. R. Ballard."

"Who wants to play it safe anymore?" he whispered against her ear, letting his full weight press into her.

"Oh, Jack. My whole world is topsy-turvy. The blood is rushing...to my head. I feel dizzy and breathless. I...can't think straight anymore."

"Yup. You've got all the symptoms, all right."

"Insanity?"

"Love."

"What's the difference?"

"One's a lot more fun."

She raised an eyebrow and gave him a cockeyed smile, "Oh, yeah? Which one?"

He'd worked her robe open again his lips finding their way to her breasts. "You decide," he whispered against a ripe, hard nipple.

Jill muffled her gasp against Jack's chest, her hands winding their way around his neck.

There was another knock on the door, this one bolder. "Oh, J.R., you're missing the very best part."

"That's what she thinks," Jill murmured hotly into J.R.'s ear.

6

AT CLOSE TO TWO O'CLOCK in the morning, Jack, clad in a pair of pj bottoms, fought back a yawn and tiptoed from his bed over to the door. Cracking the door open, he peeked into the living room to see if the coast was clear to dash into Jill's bedroom.

Well, at least the TV was off and the lights were out now. Of course, that made it almost impossible for Jack to detect if Eleanor had finally fallen asleep. Really, this wasn't at all how he'd imagined he'd be spending his first days as a married man.

He drew the door open a bit wider. It made a low whine. He moved away from the door as he heard a muted "mmmmm" from the direction of the couch. Then came some creaking springs. Eleanor rolling over. He waited nervously for more tossing and turning.

A few more intermittent creaks and then silence. After a couple of anxious minutes he finally detected Eleanor's slow, even breathing. That had to mean she was asleep. He took a cautious step outside the door. Then another. He looked toward Jill's bedroom door, trying to calculate how many more steps he'd need to take. The big problem was that Jill's room ran in a direct line across the living room from the spare bedroom. The shortest distance between the two points was a straight line that brought Jack dangerously close

to the couch. On the other hand, if he opted for taking
the long route around, he'd be under risk of exposure
that much longer.

The scientist in him, as well as the daring adventurer, chose the shortest, most direct route. As he made
his way cautiously across the living room, he felt a rush
of excitement picturing a nude Jill sprawling under the
covers, in the warm vulnerability of sleep, just waiting
for her Robinson Crusoe to crawl in beside her.

He was getting closer and closer to the couch area.
Eleanor's breathing remained steady and rhythmic. So
far so good. Almost halfway home. A cinch.

"Shhhh."

Jack didn't actually hear the sound. It was more a
vibration. The radiator hissing steam? Steam heat.
That's what he was feeling himself. Steam heat.

"Shh, J.R."

Jack froze. No radiator he'd ever heard of hissed ini-
tials. Eleanor. Oh, no. Eleanor awake.

In the murky darkness a head popped up from the
couch. "I couldn't sleep, either," Eleanor whispered.
She switched on the lamp beside the couch.

Reflexively Jack crossed his arms over his chest, fro-
zen in a ridiculous melodramatic pose and feeling exactly like a wolf caught in a trap. He gave Eleanor a
nervous, embarrassed smile.

She smiled back, seductively, his appearance in the
middle of the night confirming her suspicions that J. R.
Ballard did, indeed, harbor flattering desires toward
her. As she did toward him.

"I must look a sight," she murmured coyly.

"I was just . . . getting a drink . . . of water. From the . . . kitchen."

Eleanor grinned. "Why, J.R., the kitchen is right next door to your room."

"The bathroom. I was . . . going to the bathroom . . . first."

"You surprise me, J.R."

"I do?"

"I never dreamed you'd be . . . shy."

"Shy?"

"Oh, I am, too. Shy. Usually. Nothing like this has ever happened to me before." She swung her legs to the floor and sat up.

"Nothing like what?" Jack asked nervously.

Eleanor, clad in a virtuous high-necked flannel gown, held the blanket up to her chest in an unnecessary gesture of modesty.

As she clutched the blanket against her with one hand, she patted the cushion of the sofa with the other. "Please sit down, J.R."

"I . . . the bathroom . . ." he stammered, falling pathetically out of character.

Eleanor smiled demurely. "I'll wait."

He had to walk right past Jill's bedroom to get to the bathroom. He gave her closed door a wistful glance that was steeped in longing and the injustices of real life.

He felt embarrassed and awkward standing in the bathroom, counted in his head what he assessed to be a reasonable amount of time to spend there. He tried to regroup, but it wasn't easy, knowing that Eleanor was waiting out there in the living room with baited breath. He flushed, ran the tap, squared his shoulders, and exited.

Eleanor had used the brief time apart to run a brush through her hair, and as he got closer to the couch he picked up a whiff of peppermint. *Kissing-sweet breath.*

"Eleanor, I really have to . . ."

"Shh." Eleanor grabbed his bare arm, tugging him down to the couch. "You don't want to wake your sister, J.R." She leaned in closer. "I don't think she'd understand. Jillian's so hard-nosed and practical when it comes to men. I doubt she could ever relate to the kind of . . . instant attraction . . ."

"Eleanor . . ."

She pressed a fingertip to his lips. "No, don't say anything, J.R. I admit I'm very attracted to you, but I don't think we should move too quickly. We need to control our . . . natural instincts, get to know each other better . . . first. I'd be mortified, J.R., if you thought I was . . . an easy woman. I know it's different for a man. Especially a man like you. Women falling over you all the time . . ."

"Eleanor . . ."

"It's all right, J.R. I may not be a woman of the world, but I've read a lot of women's fiction, watched plenty of soap operas. And . . . now please, don't get the wrong idea, J.R., but I'm not . . . wholly inexperienced . . . when it comes to the opposite sex."

"Eleanor . . ."

"I haven't embarrassed you, J.R.?"

"I have to go to bed, Eleanor."

She gripped him even tighter. "I love your eyes, J.R. I feel like they can see right into my soul."

"Not really."

"Do you believe in fate, J.R.?"

Not anymore. "It's late, Eleanor."

She leaned a little closer. "I knew you'd be coming out of your bed tonight, J.R."

A bead of sweat broke out across Jack's brow. "It was a mistake," he muttered, working at her fingers which were coiled tightly around his wrist. Before he completed the task, a bright light suddenly flooded the room.

"Jack?"

At the sound of Jill's voice, Jack instantly popped up from the couch. Jill stood at her open bedroom door, radiating bafflement, as her gaze shifted from Jack to her assistant who'd popped up beside Jack.

"Oh, Jillian, it isn't . . . what you . . . think," Eleanor stammered. "We were just . . . J.R. had to go to the . . . little boys' room . . . and I . . . we were just . . . talking." She was still clutching the blanket to her chest.

Jill's eyes narrowed. She stared at Jack with such intensity, he felt a wholly unwarranted rush of guilt. "We were talking about . . . soap operas."

"I hope I didn't disturb you in the middle of a cliff-hanger," Jill said acerbically.

Eleanor giggled nervously, but as soon as Jill glared at her she cut if off mid "ha."

Jack moved quickly away from the passion-crazed Eleanor. He started toward Jill, but she raised a hand up in a stop gesture.

"I just wanted to say one thing...J.R. As long as you are a . . . guest . . . in my home, I expect you to behave with . . . propriety."

He gave Jill an amused smile. "Propriety?"

"Yes," she said in a low, menacing voice. "And that includes not prancing about half naked in front of . . . women who aren't in any way related to you."

Jack offered a contrite nod. "You're absolutely right, sis. But you see, I thought Eleanor was asleep and . . ."

"Yes, he really did think I was asleep," Eleanor hurried to repeat. She flushed scarlet because, of course, she believed she was lying through her teeth.

Giving them both dubious looks, Jill said in a tight, even voice, "Then I suggest we all return to bed—our respective beds, that is—and do just that."

Jack attempted to follow Jill into her room, but she slammed the door in his face. A moment later, he heard the lock turn.

Eleanor gave him a wilted smile as he strode across the living room, entered the spare bedroom and slammed his door shut.

THE INSTANT ELEANOR walked into the kitchen the next morning and saw Jill making the coffee, she launched into an explanation. Or at least she tried to.

"Jillian, about last night. Your brother and I were only..."

"I'd rather not discuss last night, Eleanor." Jill took two mugs off her mug rack and set them on the counter.

"Is J.R. still . . . asleep, Jillian?"

"No, J.R.'s gone."

"Gone? For good? Oh, Jillian, you shouldn't have thrown him out...."

"I haven't thrown him out." Although she'd been sorely tempted. "He...jogs. At the crack of dawn."

"Will he be back before we leave for work?"

"I doubt it."

"Oh, Jillian, you are angry."

"No, not angry. More...surprised."

"Because I'm so attracted to your brother?"

Jill shrugged.

"Okay, I admit it, I used to be a prude at one time...."

"Eleanor, you were a prude two days ago."

Eleanor smiled sheepishly. "J.R. seems to stir something...primitive...in me."

"Yes, he has a way of doing that to a woman," Jill said reflectively.

"I suppose there've been a lot of women in his life. Glamorous, sexy, uninhibited women." Eleanor's chin dropped to her chest dejectedly.

"Have some coffee, Eleanor." Jill poured two mugs and set one at the table in front of her assistant.

"What must your brother think of me? I made an absolute fool of myself last night. I've never been so...brazen, so obvious. I'm so embarrassed."

"Relax. He's used to it." Jill sat down across from Eleanor and took a sip of black coffee.

"Is there anyone...special in his life right now, Jillian?"

"Well..."

"Oh, God, there is. Of course there is. He's in love with someone else. Someone beautiful, worldly, uninhibited..."

A faint smile curved Jill's lips. "I never really saw her that way, but I suppose that's how Jack—J.R.—would describe her."

"It's serious then." Tears actually came to Eleanor's eyes.

Jill felt a flash of sympathy for the smitten woman. "You don't know J.R. the way I do, Eleanor. He's so . . . changeable."

"Well, then, maybe he'll change his mind about this other woman," Eleanor said hopefully.

"No. That isn't what I mean. What I'm trying to say is . . ." *What I'm trying to say is, keep your cotton-picking hands off my husband . . .* "J.R. is so . . . unstable, Eleanor. My bet is he won't stay in Philly long. He'll get . . . restless and move on. Just like always. You just can't depend on J.R. to stick around. And there is that other woman."

"Is she here in Philadelphia?"

Jill hesitated. "Not exactly. But who knows? She could show up."

"Do you like her, Jillian?"

"Do I like her? I guess I have mixed feelings about her."

Suddenly Eleanor reached out and grabbed Jill's wrist. "Oh, Jillian, will you help me?"

Jill swallowed. "Help you?"

"Put in a good word for me. I can give him so much, Jillian. Stability, warmth, understanding . . . passion."

"Passion?"

"Don't misunderstand me, Jillian. I certainly wouldn't do anything rash in that regard. I've already discussed that with J.R."

"You've discussed *passion* with J.R.?"

"I made it crystal clear to J.R. that I could never just . . . have an impulsive . . . physical relationship . . . with a man. And as intensely physical as I might feel about J.R., I want a . . . deeper, more meaningful relationship. J.R.'s a man of the world. Even you must realize that he's not exactly a . . ." She flushed. "Well, you know what I'm trying to say, Jillian. Women must always be inviting him into their boudoirs."

"Is that what J.R. told you? That he's an ace stud?"

"Jillian, really. J.R. is too much of a gentleman to be so . . . blunt about his . . . exploits of that nature."

Jill gave Eleanor a sympathetic smile. "Eleanor, can I give you a piece of friendly advice?"

"No, Jillian. I'd rather you wouldn't."

"Eleanor . . ."

"I love him, Jillian. There, I've said it. How can I help but love him? I know you think that's crazy."

"No."

"Yes, of course you do. How can I expect you to understand? You're far too sensible to ever let yourself fall in love at first sight. You probably don't even believe such a thing is possible."

Jill merely shrugged and rose from the table to rinse out her mug. "We better get moving or we'll be late for work."

Eleanor checked her watch. "Oh, you're right." She swallowed the last drops of coffee and carried her mug to the sink.

"By the way," Eleanor said, setting her mug on the counter while she waited for Jill to finish washing her mug, "how'd your meeting go yesterday with August and the new grant manager? What's his name? Harris? Harrison?"

Jill froze. "Harrington," she muttered.

"Right. Harrington. Jack Harrington. So, what's this Jack Harrington like?"

"Typical scientist type." Jill busied herself washing out Eleanor's cup.

"I could have guessed." Eleanor dried Jill's mug and hung it back on the wooden mug rack above the counter. "Did August tell you that he wanted me to act as liaison person between Harrington's evaluation team and our department?"

The mug Jill was washing slipped from her trembling fingers and smashed in the sink.

Eleanor looked from the broken mug to Jill's ashen face. "Oh, dear. Are you ill again, Jillian? You really must have picked up some kind of a bug on that island. I hope you didn't drink the water down there. Of course, it's almost impossible to avoid it. They rinse off all the vegetables with the water. Then, there you are, carefully drinking bottled water and eating a salad with all those droplets of water. . . ."

"Please, Eleanor."

"Maybe you should call in sick, Jillian?"

"No. I'm . . . all right."

"Are you sure? You seem awfully prone to these sudden attacks. . . ."

"I just need to get my bearings." She sat back down at the kitchen table, Eleanor hovering over her like a mother hen.

Jill's mind was racing. She simply couldn't let Eleanor work with Jack. It was one thing if the two of them hardly ever saw each other at the foundation, but if they were to get together on a day to day basis . . .

"Jillian? Are you feeling any better?"

"Not yet," she muttered.

"Are you sure you don't want to take the day off?"

"No, I can't. There's too much to take care of at work."

"I know. It does pile up when you take a vacation. But don't worry about it, Jillian. I'll pitch in all I can."

"You won't be able to . . . help me very much, if you're . . . working with . . . Harrington."

"Oh, but I won't be."

"What? But you said . . ."

"I hate working with those scientist types. They're so picky and noncommunicating and . . . well, they can really drive you up the wall."

"But August . . ."

"Oh, he wanted me to do it, but I finally managed to convince him that Paul Cook would do a better job, since he was pre-med in college and has a better understanding of the scientific mind. Pretty clever of me, huh?"

Life rushed back into Jill's face. "Very clever, Eleanor. Very clever."

"You certainly seem relieved. I guess I'm more indispensable to you than you let on, Jillian."

"I . . . guess you are." She popped out of her chair. "Well, we better hurry or we'll be late for work."

"My, that attack of yours passed quickly."

"I must have drunk my coffee too fast," Jill said airily. "I'm feeling much better now."

JILL REALLY WAS SWAMPED with work, and, amazingly enough, she managed for whole stretches of time that morning not to even think about the ever-escalating complications Jack Harrington, alias J. R. Ballard, had added to her life. They did, however, return to mind in a rush when Eleanor appeared in her office just before lunch.

"Jillian, I was just wondering . . . does J.R. like music?"

"Music? I suppose."

"Concert music? Mozart? Beethoven?"

"Why are you asking?" Jill queried cautiously.

"I thought I'd get tickets for a concert. . . ."

"He's not crazy about classical music."

"Oh. How about . . . ?"

"Eleanor, I'm really far too busy to discuss my brother's taste in music right now. And you should be too busy to be thinking about it."

"My, you are Grouchy Greta this morning, Jillian."

"Maybe that's because I didn't get a solid night's sleep."

Eleanor flushed. "Well, it won't happen tonight. I'll have a word with your brother."

"So will I," Jill said tightly.

Jack appeared at Jill's office door a minute after Eleanor's departure. There was every chance they'd passed right by each other.

His arrival set Jill's teeth on edge. "Close the door," she said sharply.

Even as she glared, silently castigating him for making her life utterly nerve-racking and chaotic, she had to marvel at his transformation from superhero back to bland, unassuming scientist.

"Good morning, Jillian." Gone was the western twang along with any other visible sign of J.R.

"What are you doing in here?"

"You just told me to come in and close the door." A wisp of a smile appeared on an otherwise bland visage.

"Before this is over, you're going to drive me stark-raving mad, Jack Harrington."

"I'm sorry, Jillian," he mumbled, but he didn't look very contrite.

She leaned forward in her seat, scrutinizing him more closely. "Are you wearing makeup?"

"Just some face powder. I thought I should tone down my tan. Too much?" He rubbed his face. "There, how's that?"

Jill raised her eyes to the ceiling.

"If it makes you feel any better, Eleanor didn't bat an eye when I introduced myself to her."

"You . . . what?"

"It would have looked rather odd if I hadn't."

She pressed her palms to her temples and closed her eyes.

"We even shook hands," Jack said brightly. "A very limp shake. I thought that was a nice touch."

"You're enjoying all of this, aren't you?"

"I thought you'd be pleased, Jillian. And, just as a quick aside, sis, about last night . . . I was on my way to your bedroom when your assistant waylaid me. I'll have to be more careful tonight."

"Don't waste your time. My bedroom door will be locked."

"Jill . . ."

"Jillian, and don't you forget it. Furthermore, as far as our working relationship goes, Jack Harrington, let's get a few things straight. One, stay away from Eleanor. Two, stay away from me. You can nod to me in the hall in passing, but that's it. I don't want you coming to my office. I don't want you coming over to my table at lunch. I don't want you sitting anywhere near me at staff conferences. And as for home . . ."

"I get the picture, Jillian."

"Good. Then you can close the door again...on your way out." She pretended avid interest in stacking papers on her desk.

Jack made no move.

Jill looked up and gave him a sharp stare.

"August wanted me to go over these grant applications with someone in your department." He held the papers in his hand as if they were exhibit A. "Actually he wanted me to talk to Eleanor about them, but I thought you'd prefer I spoke directly to you."

"I thought Peter Cook was your liaison person," Jill said suspiciously.

"Oh, he is, but he's got some work he needs to finish up before he can move into that position." Jack gave a quick smile. "However, if you're too busy, I could go and track Eleanor down."

"Sit."

He grinned. "You're beautiful when you're angry."

FOR THE REST OF THE DAY, Jill faced the fact that she wasn't going to be able to concentrate on market shares, corporate bonds, or any of her other, hopefully, well-placed investments. The foundation would survive. As things stood, thanks to a solid fund-raising program, conservative but shrewd strategies used in investing those funds, and cautious, highly selective approvals of grant applications, the August Foundation, despite a sluggish economy, continued to enjoy a rosy financial picture.

If only life could be as rosy as the foundation's finances.

At just a few minutes past five o'clock that afternoon, Jill stood at her office window postponing her return home and her inevitable reunion with her "brother" and her lovesick assistant.

As she stared down at the front path below her window, she saw a man in an overcoat carrying a small duffel bag dash hurriedly down the front path toward the street. A city bus was pulling up at its stop just outside the front gate of the foundation. Jill saw the man wave at the bus. The bus waited and the man climbed on.

It was her very own mild-mannered colleague, hurrying off to some anonymous restroom to turn himself back into her superhero, otherwise known in this particular incarnation as that dashing heartthrob, J. R. Ballard. Jill slowly shook her head. How long could he maintain this schizophrenic ruse? Surely he couldn't go on like this all week. She decided that, once she got home, she'd try again to get Jack to take a hotel room for the rest of the week. That way she could tell Eleanor that, typical of her brother's rootless ways, he'd left Philly and returned to his old girlfriend. Eleanor would be upset, but not nearly as upset as she'd be after a week of unrequited cohabitation with the irresistible J.R.

Eleanor popped into her office just as she was putting on her coat.

"Hi. I thought we might as well go home together," Eleanor said. "Let's splurge and take a cab. It won't be too expensive if we split it. Besides, the buses are so crowded during rush hour and they take forever."

The "forever" part was the issue. Poor Eleanor was biting at the bit to hurry home to the welcoming smile of one J. R. Ballard.

"You know how I feel about splurging, Eleanor. A bus will get us home fast enough," Jill countered, wanting to delay their arrival so that Jack could make it home first and have a chance to settle back into his brotherly role before Eleanor pounced. Jill had no idea how much time it would take her superhero in that phone booth.

Jill stuck some papers in her attaché case and the two women exited the office.

"By the way, Jillian, I called your brother this afternoon."

"Oh? What did he have to say?" she asked with a faint smile.

"He wasn't home."

"Well, J.R.'s not much of a homebody."

"Maybe he was job hunting."

Jill gave Eleanor a doubtful look. "I suppose it's possible."

"You can't say I'm being presumptuous, but I really think you should be more supportive of your brother's efforts to settle down."

"You can say I'm being presumptuous, Eleanor, but I think you'd be a lot better off if you accepted that my brother's a heartbreaker. And don't forget, Eleanor, there is another woman."

"She isn't right for him, Jillian. Don't ask me how I know it. I just feel it. I can see a longing in J.R.'s eyes. He's searching for something, Jillian. There's a tension in him. There are needs that woman isn't meeting. He's not satisfied. I believe J.R. is a frustrated man, Jillian."

Well, I certainly couldn't argue that one.

7

JACK SNAPPED THE EIGHT of diamonds on the nine of spades. Next card up was a jack of clubs. No red queen to lay it on. A jack and his queen belonged together. He peeked under each of the top piles of cards, found a queen of hearts, laid it face up on his bed and set the jack beside it. Pushing away the rest of the cards from his solitaire game, he stared wistfully at the jack and queen.

Three days and three torturous nights had gone by since the unexpected arrival of Eleanor Windsor. Of course, he wouldn't admit it to Jill, but he was no happier with his clever game plan than Jill was. And what was worse, Jill had decided that, since he'd made his bed, so to speak, she'd let him lie in it. Every evening, Jill came home from work, grabbed a quick bite of dinner and disappeared into her bedroom behind her locked door. She had work to do, she'd say offhandedly—so much work to catch up on due to vacation. And she'd land a few digs. More than once she reflected on whether one week in Tobago—albeit a glorious week—was worth all of the strain and drain being away had caused.

Jack was miserable. He knew Jill was pretty miserable, too. Only Eleanor seemed bright and cheery-eyed.

And why not? With Jill holed up in her room every evening, Eleanor had J.R. all to herself.

Jack continued to do everything he could think of to discourage Eleanor's infatuation, especially by confirming that, yes, there was another woman. And, yes, even though they were temporarily separated, he still held out hopes of a reunion.

Instead of Eleanor's interest diminishing, it took on ever-increasing intensity. She was impossible to discourage, her theory being, out of sight, eventually out of mind.

Little did Eleanor know how untrue that was. The less Jack saw of Jill, the more he longed for her. Every night as he lay alone in bed, trying to go to sleep, all he could think about was those passion-filled tropical moonlit nights in Tobago, Jill all flushed and steamy, her very breath the rhythm of lovemaking itself, her fine, golden skin tasting like sea spray.

Now Jack was left with a bitter taste in his mouth, and an unquenchable thirst. He shoved the cards off the bed, including the jack and queen. Then he flicked off the light and stretched out on his back.

He could hear the muted sounds of the TV in the living room. Eleanor, the night owl. Eleanor, hoping he'd slip out of his room again so she could put some of her secondhand soap opera experience into action.

Jack felt compassion for Eleanor, and even though he continued to discourage her crush on him, he did so with kindness. Someday, maybe, her own Robinson Crusoe would come along.

Rolling over onto his stomach, Jack tried to get comfortable. It was a nice-enough bed. A little narrow, but the mattress was firm. It wasn't the bed that was the problem.

Strains of laughter from the TV laugh track filtered into his room. Jack heard it as a mocking laugh. It riled and frustrated him. It didn't take much.

He could hear the padding of Eleanor's footsteps passing outside his room on the way to the kitchen. Two minutes later, the footsteps returned. Eleanor heading back to the couch. He could hear the theme music of the *David Letterman* show. Letterman would keep Eleanor company for a while, but who would keep *him* company?

Jack tossed and turned for a good half hour, the flow of adrenaline and Caribbean island fantasies making it impossible for him to settle down. Finally he threw the covers off of him, flicked on his bedside lamp and got up. It was five past one in the morning. He wrapped the blanket around him and walked over to the window, slipping and nearly losing his balance on the cards he'd scattered earlier all over the floor.

Pulling back the white linen curtains, he stared out the window at the twinkling night lights of the city. The sounds of traffic mingled with the muted drone of Letterman's opening monologue.

He thought about Jill, burrowed under her covers in the dark warmth of her bed. A bed big enough for two. A bed they'd managed to share exactly one night so far. Since then, Jill had been so edgy and distant. The magic was fading fast. And yet, Jack knew Jill loved him. He was absolutely convinced that in Tobago, Jill's real emotions—her humor, her passion, her gaiety, her warmth—had blossomed and flourished. This overwrought, tense, workaholic woman wasn't the real Jill. And Jack knew it was up to him to help her find herself again, because only then would she be able to find her way back to him.

He cursed the drone of the TV. He cursed Jill's locked bedroom door. A feeling of immediacy took hold of him as he stood at that window. He had to get to Jill. Now. Right now.

His gaze dropped and he stared thoughtfully at the two-foot-wide ledge below his window. Maybe it was closer to three feet. Then he thought about the terrace outside the sliding glass door to Jill's bedroom. He did some quick mental calculations. All he'd have to do to get to that terrace was to inch along the ledge to the corner of the building—he estimated about ten feet— turn the corner, inch along maybe another five feet, and *voilà*, he'd be at the terrace.

Maybe she wouldn't let him in, he thought with consternation. He'd refuse to leave until she did. Surely she wouldn't leave him out there to freeze in the twenty-degree temperature. To be convincing, he'd wear only his pj bottoms.

He felt a jolt of arousal imagining Jill's heated body against his chilled, shivering torso. *Oh, baby, warm me, heat me . . .*

JILL COULDN'T UNDERSTAND it. A man had shared this bed of hers for exactly one night, and yet since then it had felt oddly empty without him. Of course, it wasn't just any man. It was the man she'd fallen impossibly in love with, in a tropical island paradise. A man she'd married without a moment's thought as to what married life would be like.

Certainly no amount of premeditation would have led her to think it would be like this.

For the past three stress-filled days and even more stress-filled nights, Jill had carried out her resolve to let Jack stew in his own cleverness. She knew he was suffering under the strain. And Eleanor's overzealous attempts to woo brother J.R. were greatly adding to that strain.

Jill was feeling the strain, as well. Each evening, behind her locked bedroom door, as she stared distractedly at her work, she could hear the muted sound of Jack's voice from the living room. Even though he did disguise it with that western twang, his voice evoked sensual remembrances, longing and desire.

Jill rolled over to her side in bed away from the empty space beside her. Jack's space. In the dark she could see the lighted numbers of her digital clock. They read 1:05. Later than she'd thought. She wasn't having any easier time falling asleep tonight than she had the last three nights. Every time she shut her eyes, frustrating images of those passion-filled Tobago nights danced tantalizingly across her closed eyelids. She rolled over again, opened her eyes and stared at the empty space beside her.

JACK PINNED HIMSELF against the freezing, rough wall of the building, five stories above the concrete city sidewalk. His slippered feet were anchored to the narrow ledge. He'd been overly generous estimating its width. Before stepping out on that ledge, desperation and longing had filled Jack with a wild and reckless daring. He was Robinson Crusoe incarnate. There was no mountain high enough, no river wide enough, to keep him from recapturing his gal Friday.

But this wasn't a mountain or a river, and that five-story drop took his breath away. Shivering violently from an equal mix of wind-chill factor and terror, he prayed for his reflexes to return and for the quaking fear to leave the pit of his stomach long enough for him to moor his feet.

He considered climbing back in his window, crawling into his own narrow, lonely bed, and resigning himself to his solitary fate. But, there were times a man had to take fate into his own hands. Like he had in Tobago.

And so, despite the swarm of monumental doubts concerning the wisdom of this particular route, Jack strained against the dizzying environs of what might as well have been outer space and arduously inched along toward his siren love. With this experience in the bag, tomorrow night's repeat performance would be a piece of cake.

By the time he climbed over the half wall onto Jill's terrace, shaking and quaking, he'd sworn off cake for good.

The curtains were drawn across Jill's sliding glass door and the lights were off in her room. He knocked lightly and then pressed his lips close to the thin crack between the sliders.

"Jill. Jill . . . it's me. Jack. On the . . . terrace."

JILL SPRANG UP in bed. She blinked. Was she dreaming? She could have sworn she'd heard Jack calling out to her.

She hurried out of bed and across the room to the bedroom door. She pressed her hear to it. All she could hear was David Letterman's voice.

She sighed. For a moment, she'd thought that maybe Eleanor had fallen asleep with the TV on and Jack had decided to throw caution to the wind and try to get to her room again. Disappointment and longing enveloped her.

And then she heard Jack's voice again. Only it wasn't coming from outside her bedroom door. It was coming from . . .

She stared across the room at her sliding glass door. No. Impossible. There was no way. Had things gotten so bad that now she was hallucinating? Did she imagine that her irrepressible husband had grown wings, flown through space and alit on her terrace? Or was he really a superhero after all?

She started for the bed, thinking that maybe she should take a sleeping pill. But she didn't have any sleeping pills. She'd never before needed sleeping pills. Maybe she'd have to get some for tomorrow night.

"Jill. Please...unlock the door. I'm...freezing. And I won't . . . leave this spot . . . until you . . . let me in."

Jill moved cautiously toward her sliding glass door. If this was a hallucination, forget about getting sleeping pills tomorrow. She'd head straight to the nearest asylum and commit herself.

JACK AND JILL LOOKED at each other through the glass.

"Are you crazy, Jack?" Jill whispered. "How did you get out there?"

"I ... can't ... hear ... you." His teeth were chattering so much he could barely get the words out. So much for the sex appeal of his bare-chested arrival.

"What did you say?" Jill raised her voice a notch.

Jack rattled the door. "Let ... me ... in."

"Shhh." Quickly she released the catch and slid the door open.

Jack rushed into the room, a gust of icy wind chasing his goose bumps through the slider.

"How did you get out there?" Jill asked, dazed.

"I ... walked."

"In space?"

"The ... ledge."

"Oh, Jack, you're crazy."

"You're ... right."

She threw her arms around him.

"Oh, baby, warm me, warm me," Jack croaked. He'd intended to croon the words, but his teeth were chattering too badly to produce the desired effect.

JILL'S NIGHTGOWN LAY in a mound on the floor. Jill lay in Jack's arms on the big double bed, a bed that definitely improved with two occupants.

Jack was still shivering too badly for any serious lovemaking, but he figured they had plenty of time. Jill hugged him close, willing all of her body heat into him.

"Oh, Jill, you ... feel ... so ... good," he stammered.

"So do you, Jack. But you were nuts to risk such a stunt."

"I'd risk . . . anything . . . for you, Jill." He dipped his icy fingers between her heated thighs and she let out a little gasp. "Too cold?"

She laughed softly. "No. It feels great."

"I've missed . . . you . . . so, Jill," he murmured, tasting her with small, soft, anticipatory kisses.

"It's been a dreadful week," she admitted. "And it isn't over yet."

His kisses grew more erotic. "Don't think about that now, Mrs. Harrington."

"Mrs. Harrington," she echoed wistfully, pressing her face against his cheek, which was finally warming a little. "The secret Mrs. Harrington."

His lips found their way to her lips. Warmth began spreading down his spine, filling him with simmering waves of desire. "As long as we don't keep any secrets from each other, Jill, that's all that counts. Years from now, we'll laugh about this."

"We will?"

He stroked her back, then his hands clasped her hips, pressing her closer. "We will," he whispered.

Just when Jack was finally warmed up, or, more to the point, heated up, he and Jill heard the faint strains of Eleanor's voice calling out, "J.R.," from the living room, followed by a light rapping sound.

"Oh, my God, she's knocking on your door," Jill gasped.

"Damn, I left my light on in the room. She probably thinks I'm awake."

Jill grinned. "You are awake, darling."

"But she doesn't know that. Maybe she'll think I fell asleep with the light on and go away."

"J.R., please open the door. I think...somebody may have... broken into the apartment. I heard a rapping sound." There was a note of desperation in Eleanor's voice.

Jill gave him a little shove. "She's not going to go away, Jack. You've got to go back to your room and talk to her."

There was only one route back to his room, and to say he was dreading it, was putting it mildly. Wild horses wouldn't have gotten him out on that ledge again. But Eleanor Windsor was another matter.

"Don't worry, Jack," Jill said softly, misinterpreting his despair. "I'll leave my slider unlocked. After you calm her down, you can come back."

THE PAINTERS WHO WERE working on Eleanor's apartment phoned her at Jill's on Friday to say they'd finished the job.

"That's great. Two days earlier than you expected," Jill said, trying not to sound rudely exuberant. Just to be on the safe side, she added, "Sleeping on that lumpy couch couldn't have been too pleasant."

Eleanor merely shrugged, in no way concealing her disappointment. "I was going to help J.R. work on building you that bookcase on Saturday. And I thought Sunday, I'd make a big brunch for all of us. As a kind of thank you."

"That's sweet of you, Eleanor, but actually J.R. has never been one for brunches." Jill patted a nonexistent tummy. "And I'm watching my weight. I put on a few pounds in Tobago."

Eleanor sighed.

"Besides, this way you have the weekend to straighten up your apartment, get it organized again. Having a place painted can be so disruptive."

"I suppose," Eleanor muttered tonelessly.

Eleanor was packing her bags when Jack arrived home fifteen minutes later.

"The painters finished up early," Jill told him in a deliberately subdued voice.

Eleanor looked up from the couch. "They weren't supposed to be done until Monday."

Jack did his best to conceal his glee. "Oh...you must be thrilled."

Which of course he knew she wasn't.

Suddenly Eleanor brightened and she gave a little sparkling laugh. "Hey, I've got a great idea. Why don't you come over to my place for dinner tomorrow night?" As an afterthought, she glanced at Jill. "Both of you."

"Tomorrow night?" Jill shot Jack a quick look.

"I'm dying for you to see the apartment, J.R.," Eleanor said eagerly. "Remember how you said you loved the color rose, J.R.? Well, I did my bedroom in the most gorgeous shade of rose...."

"Tomorrow night?" Jack shot Jill a quick look. "Didn't you say something to me the other day about Saturday night, sis? Some plans you'd made for us?"

"Oh...yes. Yes, you're right."

"What plans?" Eleanor asked recalcitrantly. "You didn't mention anything all week about plans for Saturday night."

"Tickets for the 76ers' game. Basketball," Jill said in a rush. "When J.R., uh, called to say he was coming, I picked up a couple of tickets. J.R. loves basketball."

Eleanor gave him a narrow gaze. "I thought football was your sport, J.R."

"Well, basketball, too."

"Yeah, Dad used to take us to basketball games all the time when we were kids, didn't he, J.R.?"

"Yes, he did. Dad was crazy about basketball. Of course, Mom wouldn't put up with him watching games all the time on TV. Remember how she'd blow up at him, sis?"

"How could I forget?"

Jack and Jill shared sibling smiles.

"How about Sunday night, then?" Eleanor was quick to suggest.

"With work the next day?" Jill shook her head. "Not a good idea."

Eleanor brightened. "Well, you're not working, J.R."

Jack patted his chest reflectively. "No, I'm not working, exactly, but . . ."

"He's got a job interview on Monday morning."

"You're right, sis. I almost forgot. I should turn in early on Sunday night."

Eleanor closed her suitcase with a defeated little snap. "Well, maybe one night next week." She'd lost the battle, but not the war.

"Yes . . . maybe," Jack and Jill said in unison.

TEN MINUTES AFTER Eleanor's heralded departure, Jack and Jill were enfolded in each other's arms in Jill's big double bed.

"Oh, Jack, I thought we'd never be alone. Tell me this isn't a dream."

He showed her instead, stroking her breast, then cupping it, gently teasing her nipple with his thumb.

"Mmmmm. No dream is as good as this," she murmured as she felt the delicious coolness of his hand sliding down her belly.

They kissed deeply, fiercely, with the kind of hunger that came from starvation. *Starved for kisses.*

Jill flung her arms around Jack, positively wallowing in the luxury of having her husband back at last.

"I love you," she whispered, pressing into him, her curves fitting snugly, perfectly, with all his hollows.

He encircled her waist, his mouth burrowing into her shoulder, his warm breath caressing her skin. Tenderly, languorously, he kissed the pulsating hollow at the base of her throat, then began a slow, tantalizing trail from her neck to just above her breast. He took his time, letting Jill savor the sensations, savoring them himself.

She arched against him, her hands caressing his firm, golden body, her lips following the trail.

"You are my wild, exotic island princess," he murmured. Yes, he'd found her again. And he'd helped Jill find the way back to her true self.

"And you are pirate and superhero rolled into one."

"What about nerdy scientist and big brother?" he teased.

"Those are both just disguises, darling."

He gave a low groan as Jill's lips lightly grazed his stomach. Jill could feel his muscles contract with pent-up desire. She felt the same. But they shared a need to luxuriate in the privacy they had at last. They had all the time in the world now.

"Jack, is this all really going to work out somehow?"

"Of course it's going to work out. Look how well things are going at the foundation. We get to be together every day and no one's any the wiser. And there's no reason for them ever to be."

"What if someone from work sees us together . . . coming out of a movie theater?"

"They won't."

"We're not going to go to movies?"

"You're not going to go to movies with nerdy Jack Harrington from the August Foundation. You'll be going to the movies with . . . your brother, J.R. We're such close siblings. Why, we're practically inseparable." He slid on top of her. "Let me prove that to you."

But Jill wasn't quite ready. "What are you going to do about Eleanor, Jack?"

"Eleanor?"

"She's crazy about you."

"She'll get over it."

"I don't know, Jack. I've never seen Eleanor behave anything like this, and I've known her for five years. Why, she's the woman who complained to August after our last employee picnic about the men removing their shirts during the softball game. She insisted it was indecent. You walk around the apartment without your shirt and she positively salivates."

Jack grinned. "What about you?"

Jill laughed, letting her hands glide down his broad chest. "I think it's positively indecent for any man to look this good."

He draped his leg over her. "You say the nicest things." He gripped her wrists and drew them over her head.

She arched up into him, smiling sultrily. "Take me," she whispered.

Just as Jack was gleefully about to fulfill Jill's ardent request the doorbell rang.

They groaned in unison.

"It can't be," Jack said.

"No, it can't be," Jill agreed.

But they both knew it wasn't a bible salesman or the Fuller Brush man. They both knew...

"Eleanor," Jill muttered as she stared at her fuming assistant standing at the open door. Jill's eyes dropped to the suitcase in Eleanor's hand. She felt a sinking sensation.

"You won't believe this. You just...did I catch you on your way to the shower?" Eleanor stared with surprise at Jill in her bathrobe.

"Uh...yes. Yes...actually. I was just about to...step in."

Eleanor brushed past her, entering the apartment. "It's a good thing those painters were still there when I got home. That's all I can say," Eleanor muttered.

"What...happened?"

"What happened? I'll tell you what happened. Those worthless painters are totally color blind. Did I or did I not say rose for the bedroom?"

"Rose..."

"Precisely. Rose. I even gave them a swatch of material with the exact shade."

"And?"

"It's pink. They painted my bedroom pink."

"Pink?"

"Pink."

Jack ambled out of the spare room, dressed in jeans and a work shirt. "Why, Eleanor..."

"Oh, J.R., you won't believe this," Eleanor exclaimed.

"The painters painted her bedroom pink," Jill said with a sigh.

"Pink?" Jack replied, the light blinking out of his eyes.

"Pink," Eleanor confirmed.

"Well, pink is nice, Eleanor," Jack said encouragingly.

"Pink is not rose," Eleanor said severely.

"No. Well, actually there is a...connection," Jack said.

"I will not have people taking advantage of me, J.R.," Eleanor said firmly. "I'm very easygoing, very good-natured. But if someone tries to pull the wool over my eyes...well, there'll be the devil to pay."

Jill, standing just behind Eleanor, rolled her eyes.

Eleanor squared her shoulders. "I demanded that they repaint the bedroom immediately, and I told them I wouldn't pay one cent more in overtime."

"And they agreed?" Jack asked wanly, knowing it was purely a rhetorical question.

"Of course they agreed," Eleanor confirmed.

"How long did they say it would take?" This question came from Jill.

Eleanor shrugged her shoulders. "Well, a few hours. But the room has to dry before I can use it—which will take the weekend, anyway." She smiled brightly. "So now I will be able to help you with those bookcases, J.R."

"The bookcases. Oh, great."

"Well, then, smile, J.R.," Eleanor said coyly, removing her coat.

Jack fudged the best smile he could under the circumstances. The whole weekend with Eleanor. Maybe even longer. He avoided looking at Jill. It was just too painful.

"Well, I should unpack a few things," Eleanor said airily. As an afterthought, she turned to Jill and asked, "This won't put you out, will it? I mean, I was originally going to stay here until Monday, anyway."

"Put me out? Oh...no." Jill knew she wasn't sounding exactly gracious, but it was absolutely the best she could manage.

Eleanor smiled. "You're such a dear, Jillian. Isn't your sister an absolute dear, J.R.?"

Jack sighed. "A dear. Yes, sis is an absolute dear, all right."

Eleanor set about making herself comfortable in the living room. "Well, I don't know about the two of you, but I'm really looking forward to this weekend." She curled up on the couch. "Oh, Jillian, about tomorrow night..."

"Tomorrow night?"

"Yes, you better check those 76ers tickets. According to the paper, the 76ers are playing the Pistons tomorrow night. In Detroit."

"They are?" Jill forced a look of consternation. "I...must have...gotten the dates...confused."

"Anyway," Eleanor said breezily, "since you and J.R. don't have plans for tomorrow night after all, I decided I would steal your brother away for the evening."

Jill blinked. "Steal him away?"

"You don't mind, do you, Jill?" Eleanor grinned. "You two siblings aren't attached at the hip, are you?"

8

"But she said Monday at the latest," Jack muttered, nearly tripping up Jill, following her around the living room as she straightened up.

"I know. Believe me, I know," Jill retorted tensely.

"But this is Tuesday."

"I know this is Tuesday."

"Well, didn't she say anything about when those painters would be done?"

"If she had her way, they'd paint her apartment for the rest of her life."

"She's driving me crazy, Jill."

"Well, J.R., who told you to be so damn irresistible?"

"I didn't know I was going to have to be irresistible indefinitely."

"Do you think this is any easier for me? At least you don't have to sit through any of her heart-to-hearts." Imitating Eleanor now, Jill went on, "Please give me some pointers, Jillian. What is it about this other woman that J.R. finds so attractive? Why is he having such a hard time forgetting her?"

Jack cracked a smile. His first in days. "Did you tell her why?"

Jill glared at him. "No, I didn't. But she told me a thing or two."

Jack's smile blinked out. "Oh? What did she tell you?"

"She told me that you told her that I...that she...this other woman...had a habit of playing games."

"Games? I said you...she...this other woman...played games? What kinds of games?"

"She told me that you told her that...this other woman...blew hot and cold."

"Oh."

"So you did say that I...that she..."

"This other woman," Jack offered.

"So, that's what you told her? Eleanor?"

"No, Eleanor only has one temperature. Hot."

"Don't be cute, Jack."

"I'll try not to be."

"So, I blow hot and cold, do I?"

"This other woman, you mean. The one I was telling Eleanor about."

"Don't be..."

"Sorry. Blame it on frustration."

"Being cute?"

"Telling Eleanor that you...that she...this other woman...blows hot and cold."

"Jack, there's something you should know."

"Yes, darling."

"Married life doesn't seem to be agreeing with me."

"Hi, everyone. Chinese food. Come and get it," Eleanor called out cheerily as she set the bag full of white cardboard containers on the kitchen table. "Should I dish stuff out? Jillian? J.R.?"

Jill entered the kitchen and watched Eleanor unpack the containers. "You bought so much."

"We can always eat the leftovers tomorrow night." Eleanor saw Jill's bleak expression. "Don't worry, Jillian. This is my treat. After all, you've let me crash here all week. I really want to chip in."

All week? Make that close to two weeks.

"Where's J.R.? The food is going to get cold. I hope he likes some of the hot stuff. As for me, the hotter and spicier, the better."

"Yes, I know," Jill muttered.

Eleanor was too busy dishing out the food to pick up Jill's sarcastic remark. "J.R.," she called out, "come and get it."

Jack dragged himself into the kitchen.

"Oh, there you are, J.R. I was beginning to think you'd jumped ship."

The thought had crossed his mind.

Jill folded her arms across her chest. "Eleanor wants to know how hot and spicy you like it?"

"Huh?"

"The Chinese food, silly," Eleanor said with her inimitable little laugh.

"Oh. Not . . . too hot. Mild. I prefer it mild."

"Come on, J.R.," Eleanor coaxed. "Be a little daring."

"I guess I'm not the daring type."

"Of course you are, J.R. Why, you've got adventurer written all over you."

Jack gave Eleanor a tight smile. "You overestimate me."

"I don't think so," Eleanor said coyly. "Do you, Jillian?"

Jill smiled faintly. "He tried hot and spicy once."

"And what happened?" Eleanor asked.

"He's never been the same since."

Jack smiled wistfully. "Never."

IT WAS THURSDAY NIGHT. Jill couldn't sleep. Nothing new. But it was even worse tonight. It was starting to snow outside, and she was consumed with visions of passion-filled tropical nights. She put on a nightgown she'd bought down in Tobago. Jack had picked it out. Pale blue silk. Sheer, clinging, sexy.

She smiled to herself, thinking of Jack's remark on their flight home. *But I do love those nighties on you. And I love taking them off you even more....*

A shiver of arousal zigzagged down Jill's back as she stared at herself in the mirror. Then she looked over at her clock radio. Eleven-fifteen.

She tiptoed over to her bedroom door and heard Jack saying good-night to Eleanor. Eleanor, as usual, tried to coax him to stay up and watch late-night TV with her. But Jack claimed he was exhausted and made a fast retreat.

Jill leaned against her door and shut her eyes, imagining Jack in his room, getting undressed, crawling into bed. She pressed her hand to her chest. *Oh, Jack, take me, take me....*

She opened her eyes and let her gaze travel to her sliding door. She bit at the nail of her pinky. Would she ever dare ... ?

She approached the door cautiously. Pulled the drapes. Stared out to the terrace. Tried to estimate the distance to Jack's room.

She needed to get a look at the ledge, really see how wide it was. She grabbed a blanket and threw it around her shoulders. She stepped out on the terrace in her slippers, closing the slider behind her so her bedroom wouldn't get cold.

The ledge was a lot narrower than she'd imagined. How had Jack ever gotten up the courage to make the trek?

Whipped by wind and snow, Jill quickly realized the folly of her ways. Shivering, and resigned to another long, frustrating night without Jack, she went to reach for the wooden handle of her slider.

She tugged. Nothing happened. Jammed. She tugged harder. The door didn't budge. It was stuck.

She tried thumping along the edge of the door. Thump. Thump. Thump.

ELEANOR WENT OVER to the TV set and lowered the volume. Her eyes widened nervously. There it was again. Thump. Thump. Thump.

She anxiously surveyed the room. It sounded like the noise was coming from Jillian's room.

Maybe Jillian was exercising, Eleanor thought. She padded over to Jillian's bedroom door, knocked lightly. There was no response.

"Jillian?"

No answer.

Eleanor pressed her ear to the door. There was that sound again. Thump. Thump. Thump. This time there was an accompanying metallic rapping sound.

"Jillian? Jillian, are you . . . okay?"

No response.

Eleanor's hand moved to the doorknob. The bedroom door was locked. She rushed across the living room to Jack's door.

"J.R."

"I'm just climbing into bed, Eleanor," Jack called out wearily.

"Please, J.R. Open the door. Something's terribly wrong."

"Eleanor . . ."

"No, I mean it, J.R. There's a strange sound coming from Jillian's room," Eleanor anxiously whispered against Jack's door. "I knocked and . . . she doesn't answer."

"She probably fell asleep." Or was pretending to sleep, Jack thought, so that she wouldn't have to suffer through another of Eleanor's heart-to-hearts.

But Eleanor was nothing if not persistent. "J.R., you have to make sure she's all right."

"Okay, okay. Just give me a minute to throw on my robe."

When he opened the door, Eleanor immediately clutched his arm.

"Oh, Jack, something's happened to Jillian. I just know it."

"Take it easy, Eleanor." He untangled himself from her grasp.

She followed behind him to Jill's door.

He knocked. "Jill, it's me." He hesitated. "J.R."

No answer.

Eleanor clutched the back of his robe. "See, I told you. And there was this terrible banging sound." She was silent for a few moments, pressing her ear against the door. "It's gone now."

"Jill." Jack knocked louder. "Wake up, Jill." He rattled the door. "Maybe she took a sleeping pill."

"Maybe she . . . overdosed and was thumping on the floor for help. Until she . . . passed out. She's been acting very strange lately. Oh, J.R., we've got to get this door opened."

He tried once again, in all earnestness now, his own anxiety heightened.

"Something's happened," Eleanor whined behind him. "I can feel it. I can feel these things, J.R. Should I call the paramedics? The police?"

JILL REALIZED, with despair, that the catch on her sliding door had accidentally locked. There was no way she was going to get the slider open from outside. After banging on the glass for several minutes, hoping to draw Eleanor's attention, Jill gave up. With the TV on, there was little chance of Eleanor hearing her.

The way Jill saw it, she had two choices. Stay out on the terrace freezing for the next two hours or more until Eleanor shut off the TV, or climb onto the ledge and make her way to Jack's room. Considering her locked bedroom door and the chance of Eleanor falling asleep with the TV on—something she'd done several nights—Jill knew she really had only one choice. And she had to act on it in a hurry, before she was shivering so badly that she'd shiver herself right over the edge.

IT TOOK JACK four tries, and he nearly broke his shoulder in the process, but Jill's bedroom door finally gave way. He fell into the room, Eleanor practically falling in on top of him.

"Oh, my God," Eleanor gasped. "She's gone. She's been . . . kidnapped."

Jack raced to the sliding glass door. Eleanor raced into the living room and called 911.

IT WAS SNOWING HARDER now, making Jill's last few steps all the more treacherous. The wind whipped against her wet silk nightgown—she'd lost the blanket a few steps back, but she was almost there. *Oh, Jack, warm me, warm me.*

Finally she made it. Flattening herself against the facade of the building, she banged on his window.

After a couple of desperate moments she realized he wasn't in his room. And the window was locked.

Now what? she thought with despair.

"OH, OFFICER, thanks for getting here so quickly," Eleanor said with relief after flinging open the front door.

The paunchy middle-aged man in blue brushed snow off his jacket, stomped his feet on the hall mat and stepped inside. "I happened to be a couple of blocks from here when the call came in. A missing person? Is that right?"

"I think it could be a kidnapping. I heard this terrible sound coming from Jillian's room. That's Jillian Ballard, the woman who rents this apartment."

"Who are you?" The policeman pulled out a pen and a small notepad and flipped the cover open.

"My name is Eleanor Windsor."

"You live here, too?"

"Just temporarily. While my apartment is being painted. I work with Jillian at the August Foundation. Actually Jillian's my boss. And a friend."

The policeman looked over Eleanor's shoulder at Jack who was just stepping out of his room, looking perplexed and alarmed. He'd checked the ledge, first from Jillian's terrace, then from his window. She was nowhere in sight. With fear and trepidation, he'd even looked down in the street. Traffic was moving along normally. No crowds had gathered. She couldn't have fallen. So, where the hell was she?

"Who are you?" the policeman asked.

"That's J.R. John Raymond Ballard. Jillian's brother," Eleanor piped in before Jack got the chance.

"You live here?"

"Just temporarily." This again courtesy of Eleanor.

"You getting your place painted, too?"

"No," Jack said distractedly. "I just got to town." He wet his dry lips. "You didn't see anyone . . . someone hasn't . . . fallen . . ."

The policeman shook his head. "She suicidal, your sister?"

Jack looked shocked. "No. Oh, no."

"Well then, I doubt she climbed out onto a ledge five stories above the ground."

"What I think, officer," Eleanor interrupted, "is that someone broke into Jillian's room...."

"You saw someone?"

"Well, no. I mean, someone must have gotten in via the terrace."

"I've heard of second-story men, Miss Windsor, but don't you think five-story men is taking it a bit far. Or high?"

"I heard sounds. Banging sounds," she protested.

At that moment, all three of the people in the room heard a banging sound. At the front door.

The officer was the closest. He opened the door.

"I...forgot...my...key," Jill stammered. If it hadn't been for that unlocked window in the hallway, she'd still have been out on that ledge.

The officer gave the snow-covered, shivering woman in the drenched silk nightgown a head-to-toe survey. "You forgot your clothes, too. Miss Ballard, I presume?"

She nodded. Jack rushed to her with the blanket from the couch and threw it around her.

"What happened to you, Jillian?" Eleanor asked anxiously.

"Can't you see she's freezing to death?" Jack snapped. "Come on Jill, we've got to get you out of those wet clothes."

Eleanor rushed over. "Really, J.R., hadn't you better let me help your sister?"

"No," he snapped back, lifting Jill in his arms and carrying her off to her room, kicking the door closed behind him.

Eleanor gave the policeman a flushed look. "They're . . . very close."

"I guessed that," the officer said wryly.

"I'M WORRIED about your sister, J.R.," Eleanor said the next morning, cornering him in the kitchen while Jill was getting dressed for work.

"Don't worry about her. She's feeling fine now."

"No, I mean her behavior last night. What was she doing out on her terrace in the first place?"

"She couldn't sleep. She wanted a breath of fresh air on the terrace."

"Fresh air? It was below freezing out there. And it was practically midnight."

"She was . . . star gazing. She's loved looking at the stars . . . since she was a kid."

"There were no stars last night. It was snowing."

Jill walked in. "Good morning," she said crisply. "We're running late, Eleanor. We'd better hop a cab."

"Are you sure you're up to going to work today, Jillian?"

"Yes, Eleanor. I'm sure."

Ten minutes later, in the cab, Eleanor turned to Jill and gave her an earnest look. "I just want you to know, Jillian, that if something is wrong, I'm here."

"Yes, I know," Jill said morosely.

"The painters called me yesterday at work to say my apartment would be finished today, but if you'd like me to stay with you over the weekend . . ."

It took a moment for Eleanor's words to penetrate. When they did, Jill felt suddenly like she'd just gotten a thirteenth-hour reprieve. "Oh, no, Eleanor, you go on back home. I . . . I'm fine, now. Just fine. I'm going to spend a nice, quiet weekend at home." Jill's eyes sparkled.

"Well, if I were you, I'd stay in bed as much as I could."

"Oh, Eleanor, what good advice."

JACK CAUTIOUSLY OPENED Jill's office door and peered inside. "Jillian? You wanted to see me?"

Jill gave him an officious nod. "Thanks for being so prompt Jack. Could you come inside and close the door, please?"

As soon as the door was closed, Jill raced across the room and threw her arms around him. He gave her a stunned look. "My, my, Miss Ballard, what would Howard August say if he found two of his trusted employees . . . fraternizing like this?"

"How would you like to fraternize with me all weekend, Mr. Harrington?"

"Do you mean . . . ?"

"She's going home tonight. Her apartment's done."

Jack twirled Jill around, then kissed her hard on the lips. And Jill, defying all the rules and loving it, kissed him back with matching passion. They leaped apart, however, as the buzzer went off on her intercom.

Laughing, rosy-cheeked, Jill leaned over her desk to answer it.

"Jillian, Mr. August would like to see you in his office," Cynthia drawled.

"When?" Jill wondered if August's secretary could hear the breathy just-been-kissed tone in her voice.

"Right now. Unless you're involved with something important."

Jack and Jill shared smiles. "Well, I suppose it can wait . . . for a little while."

"Good," Cynthia said crisply. "I'll tell him you're on your way."

"Ah, Jillian, sit down," August greeted her effusively. "You're looking very well, my dear."

"Why . . . thank you, sir." Jill smoothed her brown tweed wool skirt as she took a seat in the leather armchair facing her boss's huge, glistening mahogany desk.

August leaned forward, resting his elbows on the desk, pyramiding his fingers thoughtfully. Jill detected a faint frown creasing his otherwise surprisingly smooth forehead.

"Is something wrong, sir?" She felt a quiver of anxiety. Since her return from Tobago, she certainly hadn't been performing at her peak efficiency. As much as she had tried to contain her anxiety, she knew she hadn't been altogether successful.

August smiled avuncularly, then pursed his lips and scrutinized her carefully. "Jillian, I'm about to embark on a new project of a sort."

"Oh?" Jill was puzzled. It wasn't like August to be vague.

"Yes. And I want you involved. In fact, I'm counting on you, Jillian."

"Well, Mr. August, you know you can always count on me."

"Good. I was confident you'd say that, Jillian. I have always felt that I could rely on you. That you would never let me down."

Jill flinched. "Never."

"I want you to come spend the weekend at my home, Jillian, so that we can discuss this project further. And there'll be some . . . people there I very much want you to meet and get acquainted with."

"This weekend, sir?" She couldn't keep the note of disappointment out of her voice.

"Yes, I'd like you to come out this evening. I've even arranged a car rental for you."

"This evening? But . . ." Her heart sank.

"I've already spoken with Eleanor. She said your slate is clean for the weekend. That you were going to stay home and take it easy."

"Yes . . . something like that, sir."

"Well, you can get plenty of rest at my place."

"It's just . . ."

"It's your brother, isn't it?" August said.

Jill's face blanched. "My brother?"

"Yes, yes, Eleanor told me your brother's staying with you for a while. Well, bring him along by all means."

"Bring him?"

"Yes, yes. I insist. I'd like to get to know your family, Jillian. And I'm sure your brother would enjoy meeting some new people. . . ."

"Well, he's . . . shy."

"Nonsense. I've already instructed Eleanor to ring him up. Eleanor will be coming along this weekend as well."

"Oh. I see."

"Eleanor already knows your brother so he'll feel quite comfortable."

Cynthia's voice came out of the intercom on August's desk. "Mr. Harrington is here for his meeting, Mr. August."

"Yes, yes. Send him in, please, Cynthia." August rose from his chair. "Why don't you finish up by noon, Jillian. Cynthia will give you the information on the car rental. I'll expect you by, say, seven tonight."

"Seven? Yes . . . seven." She rearranged her despondent expression into a suitable semblance of pleasure.

IT WASN'T LIKE Howard Wendell August to call a meeting and then be so distracted. Jack began his report again, but August broke it off.

"I'm sorry, Jack. Run that previous statement by me one more time."

Before Jack got a word out, however, August rose from his chair and raised his hand up in a stop motion.

"I'm afraid I've got some things on my mind today, Jack. Can't seem to concentrate."

"Would you like to reschedule, sir?"

Instead of an apologetic nod, August studied him with new interest. "How old are you, Jack?"

"Me? Why . . . thirty-four."

"Thirty-four." August nodded, looking down at his hands as if to give them a self-conscious appraisal. "You've done well for yourself for a man your age, Jack."

"Uh . . . yes, I suppose I have."

"Hard-working, serious, diligent, committed to your career. Fine qualities."

Jack's collar was feeling suddenly tight. "Yes, I suppose."

"No supposing about it. You should feel proud, son. I'm very pleased to have a man of your intelligence and integrity on board."

Jack shifted his neck around. "Yes. Thank you, sir."

August let out a sudden weary sigh. "I sometimes wonder, Jack, what makes one man steady and solid and another man . . . a rogue."

"A . . . rogue?" A trickle of sweat started meandering down Jack's back. He squirmed a little in his seat.

August eyed Jack thoughtfully. "I suppose you'd like to get married and have a family one day."

For an instant there was absolute silence. "A family would be nice."

Again August sighed. "I'd like that for my son, Jack. A good steady job, a wife, a family. Roots, stability, progeny."

"You have a son, sir?" No one at the foundation, including Jill, had ever mentioned anything about August having any children at all.

August's eyebrows drew together in a slight frown. "Yes. A son. Kipling."

"Does he live here in Philadelphia?"

August gave Jack a blank look, then blinked. "He's been in Paris for the last four years."

"Paris."

"Yes." There was a long pause. "Kipling fancied himself a painter."

Of all the occupations Jack would have guessed for a son of the stodgy, stuffed-shirt Howard Wendell August, an artist who hung out in Paris would have been last on his list.

It was apparently last on August's list as well.

"He's never sold anything, of course. I've never made any pretense at understanding his . . . art." August said "art" like it was an obscenity.

"Abstract?" Jack offered.

August harrumphed. "Abysmal, is more to the point." His back went ramrod stiff and he clasped his hands together. "Kipling was never really interested in art. He merely liked the affectation, and the effect it had on women. Wine, women and song, that's how my son's been spending his youth. But youth fades, my boy. Kipling was thirty-one last Wednesday. A turning point. He's finally come to see that he can't go on indefinitely without roots, without responsibility." August smiled ruefully. "Without money."

Ah, so the point turned on cold cash.

"Kipling's come home. It's time for him to settle down."

Jack wondered if the prodigal son would have agreed with that sentiment.

"Of course, it's going to be a difficult transition. What Kipling needs, Jack, is a good, solid woman. Like his mother. My Agnes is my rock, my anchor, my port in a storm. She's steady, durable, indomitable. With a strong woman at his side, Kipling could step in and take over the foundation one day."

"Yes, I suppose . . . a good woman is what every man needs," Jack muttered.

August came round the desk and gave Jack a hearty slap on the back. "Precisely, my boy. And I have just the woman for Kipling."

"You do?"

"Jillian Ballard."

Jack swallowed down the wrong tube and started coughing. August hurriedly slapped him on the back again.

"Jillian . . . Ballard?" Jack sputtered.

"You hardly know her, I realize, but surely you can see that the woman is a rock."

"A . . . rock?"

"She could have been my Agnes forty years back."

"Jillian?"

"She's the perfect woman to take my son in hand. I'm planning to introduce them this weekend."

"Jillian and Kipling?"

"Yes. I'm having a few people over to introduce my son around and start up a small project for him to undertake for the foundation. You know, to get his feet wet. And I plan to have Jillian work side by side with him. Proximity, my boy. Yes, she'll do wonders for him. And once Kipling settles down, I firmly believe he'll be a fine match for Jillian."

Jack hesitated. "Does this mean you're . . . relaxing your rule about employees fraternizing, sir?"

August gave him a look mingling surprise and indignation. "Most certainly not, Harrington. The rules of propriety that have successfully governed this foundation for over one hundred years are indurate."

"But then how can your son and Jillian . . . well, you know . . . sir?"

August's eyes narrowed. "My son is not, in the strictest sense, an employee. Yes, I plan to give him a trial run, let him head up a new project...temporarily, and certainly if he shows the mettle I'm hoping he possesses, well...there will have to be...certain adjustments."

"Adjustments?"

August gave him a dismissive glance. "If things work out between Kipling and Jillian as I hope, Jillian will have no complaints, I'm sure, about giving up her career for a happy marital partnership."

Wanna bet..., Jack mused ruefully. Aloud he asked, "Does Jillian know about Kipling?"

August winked. "No. I didn't want to make her nervous. She thinks it's strictly a business weekend."

"You mean she's staying at *your* home...all weekend? With Kipling?"

"Don't sound so alarmed, my boy. Agnes and I will be chaperoning them. And, it is, in part, a business meeting."

"You mean, there'll be some other people there as well?"

"Yes."

"From the foundation?"

"Yes."

Jack nodded slowly, his mind racing as he tried to figure out a tactful approach to get himself an invitation. There was no way he was letting his unsuspecting wife fall prey to the clutches of some professional womanizer!

"You know, Jack, I was just thinking. If you're free this weekend, perhaps you'd like to come out to the house and meet Kipling. A woman's important, but a good, solid man that my son can relate to might be just the ticket."

Jack shot up and shook August's hand. "Just the ticket, sir. Exactly what was running through my mind, believe it or not. I'd love to come."

August was a bit taken aback by Jack's exuberance, but he was also pleased. "Seven o'clock, tonight. I appreciate this. I think you and Kipling might hit it off."

"I think so, too, sir. I'm going to make every effort this weekend to form a relationship."

August gave Jack's shoulder a squeeze. "Well now, you don't want to monopolize all of Kipling's time. We do want Jillian and Kipling to…get acquainted as well, don't we?"

Jack fabricated a smile. "Oh, right, sir. Jillian and Kipling."

August put an arm around Jack's shoulder and escorted him to the door. "It's going to be a grand weekend, Jack. You're going to like Kipling. And what's more important, I believe Jillian will find him quite appealing. For all my son's faults, he's a very charming and devilishly handsome man. Quite irresistible, so the ladies say. Actually it's gotten Kipling into some sticky situations at times." He winked at Jack. "But with Jillian's help, my boy, that's all about to change."

9

"YOU CAN'T BOTH GO," Jill protested, stuffing a grey wool sweater into her suitcase.

"Okay," Jack said, handing handing her a white turtleneck jersey, "tell August your brother couldn't make it."

Jill refolded the turtleneck and sighed. "Don't you get it, Jack? It's a command performance. August made it clear he wants to meet my brother."

"Oh, I get it, all right. August wants to make sure your brother isn't some creep or halfwit before he marries you off to his only son."

"Jack, you're being ridiculous. Obviously I can't marry August's son. A small matter of bigamy."

"And you can't tell August you're already married. A small matter of unemployment."

Jack went off to the spare room to dig out a suitcase. Jill followed him.

"What are you doing?"

"Packing," Jack said succinctly.

"For which one of you?" she asked warily.

Jack shot her a narrow look. "For both of me."

"Jack..."

"I figure this way I can cover all bases. When big brother J.R. isn't on the job, good old Jack Harrington can keep an eye on things."

150   *Jack and Jill*

"On me, you mean. Me and Kipling August."

"What a name," Jack muttered. "Talk about affectation. What do you think they called him as a kid? Kippy? Kipper?"

"You're jealous of a man I've never even met."

"August says his boy's a rogue. Women find him irresistible."

"Really?" Jill tilted her head coquettishly just to irk Jack.

It worked. Jack started throwing underwear into his suitcase. "You want me jealous. Pay back."

"Pay back?" She smiled innocently.

"Don't be cute."

"Okay, then don't be crazy," she retorted, grabbing hold of his sleeve. "Look, Jack, even Superman couldn't be Clark Kent *and* Superman at the same time. I think the best thing is for both of you to beg off. I'll tell August that J.R.'s home sick with the flu, and you can phone him and say you…Jack Harrington, you…were called out of town on a . . . family emergency. That will be safer all around."

Jack kept packing.

"You'll never pull it off, Jack." She certainly didn't mean it to sound like a challenge, but she saw the spark ignite in Jack's eyes and immediately regretted her words. However, before she could come up with another approach to get him to back down, the doorbell rang.

"Oh, perfect. It's Eleanor," Jill moaned. "She figured the three of us could ride out to August's place together."

Jack grinned. "You mean the four of us."

JACK WOULD NEVER HAVE admitted it to Jill, but that first meeting between J.R. and Howard Wendell August had him more than a bit worried. It was one thing for J.R. to pull the wool over Eleanor's starry eyes, but Howard Wendell August might be another matter, indeed. What if the *august* head, as it were, of the August Foundation spotted some similiarities between Jill's rakish brother, J.R., and his shy, reserved employee, Jack Harrington? Jack knew what would happen. He'd *fall down, break his crown* ... or Jill, tumbling down after him, would break it for him.

Jack hung back from the door with nervous expectation as Eleanor rang the bell at the August mansion, a large brick three-story affair with thick white pillars, slate roof and fieldstone walls. Howard Wendell August's grandfather, Josiah August, the founder of the August Foundation, had had the house built in the mid 1800s. While it deliberately lacked any features that smacked of ostentatiousness, it was well-designed and impeccably maintained.

Jill stared straight ahead at the door, waiting for it to open. She wore the kind of sober expression one wears at a funeral. She felt like she was attending a funeral. Her own.

A manservant appeared, a dark-haired reed-thin man wearing black trousers, white shirt and white jacket.

"Please come in. The family is in the front parlor." He spoke with just the right mixture of pleasantry and command.

Jill and Eleanor each set down their one suitcase. Jack had two, a black leather suitcase and a brown one.

"This case—" Jack extended the brown one as he addressed the manservant "—belongs to Mr. Harrington. Perhaps you can take it to his room. He'll be along a bit later."

Eleanor gave Jack a baffled look. "How did you come to have Harrington's suitcase?"

Jill knew the answer to that one, but wondered how Jack was going to wiggle out of the truth.

Jack smiled pleasantly as he took off his lined leather bomber jacket. "The fellow stopped by the apartment late this afternoon, looking for Jill. He knew she was planning to drive out here, so he wondered if she wouldn't mind sticking his case in the trunk and bringing it with her. He's taking the train out later and didn't want to have to lug a suitcase along. Jill wasn't home, but I told him it wouldn't be any problem." He handed his jacket to the manservant. "Harrington seemed like a nice guy."

Eleanor gave a disinterested shrug. "I suppose. I hardly know him."

Jill shot Jack a grim look. Jack smiled brightly, a defense against his own mounting nervousness.

Howard Wendell August exited from the parlor and stepped into the hall, greeting his three arrivals with effusive cheer.

"And you must be Jill's brother, J.R.," August said, extending a hand to Jack after politely smiling at the two women first.

Jack took August's hand and nodded, a bit too nervous to risk speaking just yet.

Jill held her breath watching August angle his head back and slightly to the side as he scrutinized J.R. Jack wasn't breathing much himself.

"I don't know," August said slowly, frowning a little.

Jack extracted his hand from August's clasp. His palm was getting sweaty.

Jill's face paled and she could feel herself slide precipitously into panic.

August pursed his lips. "I don't see a family resemblance, really."

"Oh, it's there. The shape of the eyes, the bone structure," Eleanor, bless her heart, piped in.

"Mmmm," August nodded. "I suppose you're right, Eleanor." He smiled at Jack. "It's nice of you to come, J.R. I hear you're thinking of settling in Philadelphia. Not a finer place anywhere to settle down and establish roots. I've been discussing that very point with my son." August stopped abruptly and zeroed in on Jill. "Did I tell you my boy Kipling's come home from Paris?" He didn't wait for a response or even a reaction. "Come, all of you, and meet my family, have a cocktail. Harrington called a little earlier to say he'd be detained until later this evening. We'll go ahead with our dinner plans and hopefully he'll get here in time to join us for coffee and dessert."

Jill shot Jack a tight smile as August led the way to the parlor. Agnes August and her son, Kipling, rose from the brown leather sofa as Howard and the others entered the stately parlor, which bore a remarkable resemblance in both furnishings and accessories to the reception room at the foundation. Perhaps old Josiah August had cornered the mahogany and leather market!

The only jarring addition to the stately room was Kipling August. Talk about a bull in a china shop. It was hard to believe the tall, attractive, blond man with the randy smile and blue bedroom eyes grew up in this stuffy mausoleum of a house, the progeny of Howard Wendell August and his prim wife, Agnes, a small, fine-boned woman with a Queen Elizabeth hairdo and a nervous, pinched expression. And this, Jack thought, observing Agnes August, was the woman Howard August had earlier compared to his own divine Jill? While he took sharp but silent exception to the comparison, it did calm Jack down somewhat. Any man who saw a similarity between Agnes and Jill, even when Jill was in her drab Lois Lane disguise, obviously wasn't going to win any prizes for perceptiveness. J. R. Ballard and Jack Harrington just might pull this one out of the bag.

Agnes smiled a polite greeting from her position by the couch, but Kipling crossed the room, sauntering with just the right offhand elegance, to welcome his visitors. As he took each of the guest's hands in turn, starting with Eleanor, then Jack, and last, but clearly not least from the glint in his blue eyes, Jill, he gave a whispered, "Bonsoir."

Jack felt like gagging, but he noted with dismay that the two women seemed modestly charmed by the affectation. Jack's own greeting in response held an extra-heavy dose of western twang.

Agnes suggested to Howard that he offer drinks to
their guests. A minute later she suggested to her son,
Kipling—she may have once called him Kippy or Kipper, but now it was Kipling, said with nervous endear-
ment—that he offer their guests the hors d'oeuvres set
neatly and blandly on a silver tray atop the mahogany
buffet. It turned out that Agnes August preferred to
communicate indirectly through her husband and son.
She would say such things as, "Kipling, perhaps Jillian
would prefer something nonalcoholic for a refill," or
"Howard, dear, would you like to announce that dinner is ready," or "Kipling, do ask our guests how they
like their meat done."

Neither Howard nor Kipling seemed to find this
quirk of Agnes's odd, and Eleanor was oblivious, her
attentions focused mainly on J.R., but both Jack and
Jill found Agnes's indirect way of conversing quite dis-
concerting. Neither of them were sure exactly how to
communicate with her in turn. Should they say,
"Howard, do tell Agnes that the meat was done to a
perfect turn," or were they expected to speak directly
to Agnes, ignoring the fact that she'd respond via her
conduits?

That was the least of their worries, however. More
pressing was the anticipated arrival, at some point that
evening, of Jack Harrington. Jack had a plan in mind,
but it required the right timing and some fancy leg-
work. The timing was not right just yet.

A more immediate concern of Jack's was Kipling
August. Much to Jack's consternation, Kipling, who
asked them all to call him Kip, was displaying an immediate attraction to Jill. Whether he, like Jack, was

truly smitten or merely wanted to return to the family's good graces and bank account, wasn't clear to Jack. What was clear was that he found Kipling's obsequious and flirtatious manner damn irritating. Jill, however, showed no signs of minding in the least. As for Howard and Agnes, they were clearly delighted. And, to a lesser extent, so was Eleanor.

With Kip occupying Jillian so completely, Eleanor figured she could capture all of J.R.'s attention. Or at least she was determined to make every effort. Secretly she worried that J.R. was far too preoccupied with his sister. It would do them both good, Eleanor decided, if Jillian found herself a beau. And from the looks of it, she had. Admittedly Eleanor did experience a momentary flutter of envy. Not that she personally found Kip more attractive than J.R., but there was no doubt Kip would one day be stepping into his father's shoes. Before falling madly in love, Eleanor would have gladly settled for a spot on the social register.

At the dinner table, August arranged the seating so that Kip and Jill sat together on one side of the table, Jack and Eleanor on the opposite side, he and his wife at either end. It turned out, save for the supposedly missing Jack Harrington, this small group comprised the entire weekend gathering. Before dinner was served, August announced that he was bringing his son into the foundation to oversee a new department that would administer grants for worthy artistic projects.

"Of course," Howard said firmly, "these projects would have to involve some social merit."

"I suppose," Kip replied with a teasing glint in his eyes, "that graffiti artists needn't apply."

August gave Jill a nervous glance. "I'm counting on your guidance and good judgment to help Kipling along." He checked his watch. "I'm eager for Kipling to meet Jack Harrington as well. Harrington's got off to a terrific start with the foundation. I think he'll be an excellent role model for Kipling."

Kipling gave a desultory smile. "I can't wait to meet him."

Jack grinned. "Hey, Kip, you never know. Maybe the two of you will really hit it off."

Jill's face betrayed her irritation for a moment, but she quickly masked it.

"So, Kip," she said airily, shifting in her seat, "you must be excited about all this."

Kip's smile was nothing if not seductive. "It might be more exciting than I expected."

During dinner, Kipling held court, regaling the group with anecdotes about his bohemian artist days in Paris, his collegiate exploits at Yale, his childish pranks at boarding school. While his stories were told to everyone at the table, they were clearly meant to entertain and amuse Jill.

Throughout Kipling's endless discourse, Jill maintained a pleasant, interested smile, hiding her boredom out of politeness and a perverse desire to get Jack's goat. A little jealousy, worn on the other shoe for a change, gave her some small satisfaction.

"Remember that time, at Exeter, Dad, when I was suspended for mooning the headmaster?" Kipling was saying with a wicked smile.

August gave his son a severe look and turned immediately to Jill.

"Kipling was admittedly an unruly child, but, of course, it was evidence of his spunky, independent nature."

Agnes cleared her throat in a genteel manner and addressed her husband. "And don't forget to tell Jillian, dear, that Kipling had that thyroid imbalance, which I'm certain affected his behavior during childhood."

Howard scowled. "The boy's perfectly fit, Agnes," he admonished. "Always was as healthy as an ox. That doctor you took him to was a quack."

Agnes tinkled a nervous laugh. "Why, Howard dear, your own sister recommended him to us."

Howard harrumphed, as if that fact merely proved his point.

Kip leaned closer to Jill. "My poor mother is forever worrying over me, Jill. May I call you Jill?" he asked seductively. "Or do you prefer Jilly?"

"She prefers Jillian," Jack answered sharply.

Eleanor gave Jack's shoulder a little squeeze. "But J.R., you call her Jill."

Jack flushed. "That's different," he muttered. "I'm . . . family."

Eleanor smiled at Kip. "Poor J.R. is forever worrying over his sister, just like your mother worries over you, Kip."

"I do not worry over Jill . . . Jillian," Jack protested defensively. "I just . . . happen to know her likes and her dislikes."

Kip smiled disarmingly at Jill while addressing Jack. "So tell me, J.R., what are some of Jilly's likes and dislikes?"

Jack could feel a hardening of the muscles of his face. *The bastard! Jilly, indeed!* "Maybe you should ask Jillian yourself," he said archly. He was so upset he even forgot to add the western twang. No one appeared to notice.

Kip inclined his head at a roguish angle, his blue bedroom eyes swallowing up Jill. "Your brother does worry over you, doesn't he?"

Jill grinned. "You know how big brothers are."

"Being an only child, I don't." Kipling August took things quite literally. For an artist, he lacked a certain imagination.

"I can tell you, Kipling, that Jillian likes honesty, sincerity, integrity," Howard August offered, with a reproving look to his son, the message clear. *If you want this woman—as well as a return to our good graces— now is the time to shape up.*

Jack watched in outraged silence as Kipling nervily placed his hand over Jill's. "Admirable likes, Jilly. And what don't you like?"

"Chocolate ice cream."

Everyone laughed. Except Jack.

"WELL, SHALL WE ASK our guests to retire to the parlor for coffee, dear?" Agnes asked her husband after a few tidy dabs with the starched linen napkin at the corners of her mouth.

Howard did a quick check of his watch. "I was hoping Harrington would get here before we had our coffee."

"Maybe he got...tied up, and he won't be able to get down here after all," Jill said, surreptitiously casting a pleading glance at Jack.

"I certainly hope not," August said gruffly. "Harrington knows I'm particularly keen on having him meet Kipling. Besides, if a man makes a commitment, he should keep it."

Jack flashed a superhero grin at Jill. "Don't worry about Harrington," he said, turning to Howard August. "He made it clear when he dropped his suitcase off at Jill's that he'd get here tonight come hell or high water."

August rose from the table, all of the others following suit. "Why don't the women go ahead to the parlor while the men adjourn to my den for a smoke first? One cigar a day is all Agnes will allot me. And I like to save it for after dinner. Kipling? J.R.?"

Kipling smiled benignly. "I've quit cigarettes, but I wouldn't mind one of your imported cigars, Dad."

J.R. rubbed the back of his neck, looking uncomfortable. "I'm afraid, Howard, I'm terribly allergic to smoke. And, to tell you the truth, I think I'm coming down with a bit of a cold. I thought I'd turn in if you all wouldn't mind."

"Oh, J.R., it's barely nine-thirty," Eleanor protested.

"You do look a bit peaked," Jill said, pressing her hand to Jack's cheek. She may have balked about this harebrained dual impersonation of his, but she couldn't just stand by and not help him out.

Jack pressed his hand over hers and gave her a smile that wasn't exactly brotherly. Fortunately no one but

Jill could see his face as he'd turned away from the others.

"Does he have a fever?" Eleanor asked anxiously.

"Yes, I think so. Just low grade, but a good night's sleep will be just the ticket," Jill said firmly.

"By all means, Howard, we should let the boy get to bed," Agnes piped in.

"Yes, yes, of course," Howard said.

"Why don't I show you to your room?" Kip offered.

"Thanks." Jack put a brotherly arm around Jill. "Don't you stay up too late, sis. You're coming down with the sniffles yourself."

"Well," Eleanor remarked obsequiously, "it's no wonder after that little exploit on the ledge of your building in the middle of a snowstorm the other night, Jillian."

Jill gave Eleanor a hardened glare.

"Sounds interesting," Kip said with a smile.

Howard Wendell August scowled. "What's this all about, Jillian?"

"It's . . . nothing," Jill muttered, her cheeks flushed. Lady Godiva on a windy day couldn't have felt more exposed.

"Eleanor likes to dramatize things," Jack pitched in.

"Well, I . . ." Eleanor began.

"If Jilly would rather not discuss it," Kip said smoothly, "we'll just drop it."

Jill smiled gratefully at Kip. Jack's mouth twitched. He peevishly felt that he deserved at least an equal smile.

"If you're ready, J.R., I'll show you to your room," Kip said.

After thanking Agnes for a lovely meal, Jack followed Kip out of the dining room.

"I like your sister, J.R.," Kip said as they walked up the wide curved staircase to the second floor.

"So I noticed," Jack muttered.

Kip laughed. "What's so funny is, I was fully prepared not to like her."

"Oh?"

"Yes, Dad's been pitching Jillian Ballard to me practically since I landed at the airport. What a fine woman she is. How clever, responsible and reliable she is. I expected a drab, dowdy spinster."

Jack wet his dry lips. "Well, not that I don't adore my sister, but she's not exactly...a femme fatale," Jack lied.

"With a few minor alterations, she could be," Kip countered. He smiled broadly at Jack. "You're her brother, J.R. You probably can't see beyond the prim, proper appearance, but let me tell you something neither you or a man like my father would notice. There's fire in Jilly's eyes. If she ever decided to let her hair down, man, there'd be sparks flying all over town."

Jack's blood was starting to boil. "Jill has no desire to set off sparks." *For anyone but me.*

"I know this is bound to tee you off, being her brother, but I don't think you know the real Jilly." Kipling opened the door to Jack's room. Jack was plenty teed off, but he let it ride. Right now he had other fish to fry.

"Oh, your butler must have gotten my suitcase mixed up with Harrington's," Jack said casually, pointing to the black bag he'd deliberately told the manservant was his. Kipling, however, wouldn't know that.

"No problem. Harrington's is right next door. I'll make the switch."

"No, no. Don't bother. I'll take care of it. You go join your dad for that cigar."

Kipling smiled, and Jack knew it wasn't his father's cigar he was looking forward to. It was a chance to get better acquainted with *Jilly* now that big brother wasn't going to be breathing down his neck.

Jack smiled back pleasantly. "Well, goodnight then. I hope your folks won't mind if I sleep in tomorrow. I never eat breakfast."

Kip's smile deepened. A whole morning alone with Jilly... "Sleep as late as you want, J.R."

JACK CHECKED HIMSELF out in the mirror. Hair slicked back with no part, owlish eyeglasses in place, dreary blue suit, heavily starched white shirt, rep tie. He slipped on his gray wool topcoat, wrapped his gray-and-black striped scarf around his neck and gave himself one final look. It was a frown.

The problem was, how did he get outside without being observed? He knew August and son were in the den and very likely the door was closed so as not to let the acrid cigar smoke filter through the house. The women were back in the front parlor. Jill would see that they stayed put. That left the cook, who would be cleaning up the dinner dishes and making coffee in the kitchen, and the butler. The butler was the problem. He could be anywhere.

Jack looked out the window of his room. It was a long jump down to the ground. And there were no trellises or drainpipes offering an easy climb.

He peeked out the door of his room. No one in sight. No footsteps. All he had to do was make it down the stairs, across the front hall and out the door without being spotted.

Taking a deep, steadying breath, Jack started down the stairs, peering over the railing to make sure no one popped into the hallway. So far, so good.

He picked up his pace so he got to the bottom of the stairs. All that was left was about twenty feet of hallway space to cross to the front door.

He practically had his hand on the doorknob when he heard footsteps behind him. There was no place to hide. Jack swung around only to see the butler crossing from the parlor to the dining room.

If only I really were a superhero, Jack thought despairingly.

The butler gasped as he saw the strange man at the door.

"Oh . . . hello," Jack stammered. He was about to make some lame comment about the door having been unlocked. But no one in this neighborhood ever left their doors unlocked.

The surprise on the butler's face shifted to alarm and then menace. "How did you . . ."

Suddenly Jill darted out of the parlor. She smiled demurely at the butler. "It's all right. The Augusts are expecting Mr. Harrington. I let Jack in. I saw him heading up the walk when I was coming out of the powder room. I was just about to let everyone know he'd arrived." She rushed over to Jack. "We...we thought you might not...make it, Jack. I'm afraid we've all finished eating...here, take your coat off. We were just about to have dessert and coffee." She turned back to the butler who continued eyeing Jack suspiciously. "Will you tell Mr. August and his son that Jack Harrington has arrived? I believe they're in the den. Come on, Jack," she said pleasantly, "I'll take you into the parlor and introduce you to Mrs. August."

The butler gave a faint shrug, a formal nod, and went off to carry out Jill's request.

Once the butler was out of sight, Jill shot Jack a woeful grimace. "That was far too close for comfort, Jack Harrington," she admonished. "If I were you, I'd have my coffee and dessert, say a quick hello to everyone and then make an equally quick and permanent exit. You're so clever, I'm sure you'll come up with a brilliant excuse."

"Really, Jillian," Jack said with mock reproof. "A commitment is a commitment, as our esteemed host would say." A sparkle lit up his eyes. "For better or worse..."

10

HOW DID I GET MYSELF into this? Jill wondered. For the
past twenty-four hours, her dismay mounting with the
ticking away of each hour, she'd watched her phony
brother cum colleague—not to mention cum husband—do an incredible number of quick changes.
Houdini himself would have been impressed. Only Jill
wasn't so much impressed as distraught. She was terrified that at some point, either Jack would slip up or
someone at the August home would get suspicious of
the fact that Jack Harrington and J. R. Ballard never
seemed to appear at the same place at the same time.

Jill's nerves were rubbed raw, and to add to her anxiety, Kipling August seemed intent on making a play for
her. Normally she wouldn't have had any difficulty
holding off Kip's amorous advances, but with Jack, in
one of his two personas, constantly hovering over her
to make sure Kip didn't get to first base, Jill was too
keyed up to handle so much as a broken fingernail.

At six-fifteen on Saturday evening, Jill was trying to
compose herself while dressing for dinner. She wasn't
doing a very good job of it, when she heard a knock on
her door.

"Who is it?" she asked warily, expecting to hear either brother J.R.'s western twang or Jack's affected,

deliberately stilted scientist's drone. She was in for a surprise. But what else was new?

"It's Kip. Can I speak to you for a moment, Jilly?"

Jilly. She'd asked Kip at least a dozen times not to call her that. "I'm dressing, Kip. I'll see you downstairs."

"Please, Jilly. Throw a robe on or something. I won't keep you long."

"Oh…all right. Just a sec…" Still in her slip, she put on her plaid flannel robe and knotted the tie firmly.

When she opened the door, Kip smiled brightly, a shock of blond hair falling rakishly over his forehead like a paintbrush. He quickly stepped into her room, moving toward her. Reaching out a hand he touched her hair. She hadn't yet put it up in her tidy French knot. "You should always wear your hair loose like this. It does wonders for you," he murmured.

Jill immediately began pulling those giveaway strands back off her face. "I … never wear it … down. Too messy. I don't like looking … unkempt," she said pedantically.

Kip shut the door behind him. "Have you noticed that I never seem to get a moment alone with you, Jilly?"

"Really?" She gave him the kind of blank smile you reserve for the postman.

He reached out again, this time putting both his hands on her shoulders, and looked her slowly up and down. "Yes. If your brother isn't breathing down our necks, that dreary, boring scientist, Harrington, always seems to manage to worm his way in between us and go on endlessly in that flat monotone of his about his work at the foundation. I can't believe my father actually wants me to take pointers from that tiresome boob."

For all her own anger at Jack, she was not about to let anyone else criticize her husband. "He is not a boob," she said so sharply that Kip gave her a funny look.

"You don't . . . like the fellow, do you?"

Jill swallowed hard. "No." Pause. "Yes." Pause. "He . . . means well. And he's very . . . well-meaning." She shut her eyes. She knew who the boob was in this farce. Her.

Kip didn't seem to think so. He gave her a warm, conciliatory smile. "Okay, okay, sorry I put him down. If you like him, Jilly, I'll give him a chance. I'll try to get to know him better."

"No." Pause. "I mean . . . you probably wouldn't have much . . . in common with him."

"That's not altogether true." Pause. "We have one thing in common. You."

"Me? What do you mean, me?"

"I think that poor fellow, Harrington, has a bit of a crush on you, Jilly. Don't tell me you haven't picked up on it?"

"No. No, there's nothing to pick up on. I . . . I hardly know him. I mean, I know him at work, but that's it. There's nothing between us . . . Jack and I . . . or between . . ."

"Hey, take it easy. I didn't think there was anything mutual between you and Harrington. He's certainly not your type."

"What's that supposed to mean?" she asked defensively, and then tried to tone it down with a look of vague curiosity.

"You need someone with more...life, more...spirit, Jilly." He smiled sheepishly. "More physical vitality."

Jill stepped nervously away. "Really, Kip, you shouldn't talk to me that way."

"Why is that, Jilly?"

Because I'm a married woman. That's why, you boob! "We hardly know each other, Kip," she said crisply, grabbing some pins from her bureau and securing her hair. Before she turned back to Kip, she put her glasses on and tried to look as austere as the most exemplary spinster schoolmarm. "I have to confess something to you, Kip."

His expression took on eagerness and excitement. "Yes, Jilly? You can tell me anything."

She folded her hands in front of her and eyeballed him in much the way you would a recalcitrant child. "I know why you're doing this, Kip."

"Doing what?"

Jill lost a fraction of her composure. Was Kip just dense or did he want to embarrass her? "I think you're trying to make me think—" this wasn't coming out clearly, but then she hadn't had a moment of clarity practically since she'd gotten married "—that you have more feelings for me than you do."

Kip looked puzzled. "Are you trying to say that . . ."

"Yes."

"I do have those feelings for you, Jilly."

"No, you don't."

"Yes, I do," he said earnestly.

"No. Your father's the one . . ."

Kip wore a shocked expression. "My father has a crush on you, too?"

"Good heavens, no. No. Kip, please. What I'm trying to say is that I know your father would like to see you...me...the two of us...get...involved...with each other."

He smiled, showing bright white teeth. "Would you believe this is the first time my father and I have ever seen eye to eye?"

"Really, Kip . . ."

"It's true," he said, blinking his pale lashes. "I told your brother I was sure my father was trying to pawn me off on some perfectly dreadful and desperate middle-aged spinster, and I couldn't believe my good fortune when I actually saw you. I felt something snap, right here," he said, thumping his chest with his index finger.

"You told all that to...J.R.?" Jill asked nervously. No wonder he was behaving like an impossible bloodhound.

"Oh, yes." Kip smiled crookedly. "I don't think he was pleased."

"No," Jill muttered, "probably not."

"I know your brother is a bit leery of me. But honestly, Jilly, I can understand how he feels. If you were my sister, I'd want to make sure you didn't fall into the hands of some ne'er-do-well. But I really do want to settle down and take a hand in the business. Once J.R. sees that I'm serious and responsible, I'm sure I'll win him over," he said with boyish confidence.

"I wouldn't count on it."

Kip grinned. "But first, it seems, I must win you over, Jilly." He gave her a rakish smile and started across the room toward her again.

"I think you'd better leave now, Kip" she said sharply, stepping back. "I really do need to finish getting dressed for dinner. Your mother told your father she'd like us all down for before-dinner cocktails at seven."

"Jilly..."

"Please, Kip. You really must leave."

But he kept right on advancing. "Just tell me one thing, Jilly. Do I stand a chance?"

Jill wanted to give him a stern, unequivocal *no*, but she was well aware an outright rejection would not sit well with August senior, so she smiled politely and said primly, "I'm afraid, Kip, I take things like this very slowly and cautiously. I've just never been one to act...impulsively. Especially in personal relationships." If there really was any truth to the Pinocchio tale, her nose would be a good inch longer now.

Kip reached out and clutched her hand. "I understand, Jilly. That's fine. That's just fine. I won't rush you."

"And...I have my...brother...to consider, Kip."

"Don't worry about your brother," Kip said with a golden confidence. "You just leave everything to me."

Suddenly his hand came up to her neck. "Oh, Jilly, can I kiss you? Just once."

"No." It was a stern, unequivocal and very male *no* coming from an irate J.R., who'd just thrown Jill's door open.

"Ja...J.R.," Jill gasped, stunned.

"Hey, take it easy, big brother," Kip soothed.

"You're the one that needs to take it easy, Kipper. Or maybe what you need is a cold shower, better still," Jack said with low menace.

Kip's cheeks went pink and his sandy lashes blinked overtime.

"For heaven's sake, J.R.," Jill said with barely controlled fury, "will you stop carrying on like some irate . . ."

"Big brother?" Jack finished, giving Jill a glowering stare. "I'm glad Mom and Dad aren't here to see you carrying on in your bedroom with a man you hardly even know. I'm very disappointed in you, Jill."

She wanted to wring her husband's neck right there and then. But Kip, so intent on trying to win favor with brother J.R., started babbling on about how this was all his fault, and all he'd wanted to do was tell Jill that he thought she was a fine, wonderful woman, and he swore up and down that nothing improper had taken place.

Jack pressed his hands to his temples. "This whole affair has brought on one of my migraines. I've got to go lie down." His voice had an edge of tragedy in it. "Jill, you'll have to offer my excuses to the Augusts. You know how these headaches get. I'll be laid up for hours."

Jill glared at him. She was beyond feeling angry. This whole insane charade had gone on long enough. "J.R., I think the best thing for you do is to pack up and go back home tonight," she said tightly.

"Don't be too hard on big brother, Jilly," Kip said in a humoring way. "Can't you see he's really suffering?"

He's suffering? I'm the one that's in a tailspin. "Kip, would you please leave so that I can have a word alone with my brother?"

Jack winced. "Not now, Jill. This migraine is wicked. I'll come downstairs later this evening and we can talk then."

Kip gave Jack's shoulder a sympathetic pat. "Let me get you something for that headache, J.R.. Aspirin? Something stronger?"

"Thanks, Kip. Aspirin might help . . . a little."

In silent fury, Jill watched the two men exit her room. *She* could feel a legitimate migraine coming on. Was it any wonder?

"WHERE ARE YOU GOING, Eleanor?" Jill asked as her assistant started from the dining room after dinner.

"Up to see how J.R. is feeling. Maybe he'd like me to bring him up some dinner."

Jill shot up from her seat. "Oh, no. He . . . never eats when he's got one of his migraines. Makes him . . . nauseous."

"Oh, I know just how he feels," Jack murmured.

Jill flashed him a rueful glare.

"Do you get migraines, too?" Howard asked.

"Not very often," Jack said. "But, the best thing, when they do come on, is to try to sleep them off." He smiled shyly at Eleanor. "That's probably what J.R. is doing right now. I don't think it would be wise to wake him."

"Absolutely not," Kip agreed readily. "Let him sleep."

Jack couldn't help a faint grin. Poor Kip was figuring that with J.R. safely tucked into bed he'd have a second go at his sister. But Kip still had stuffy Jack Harrington to contend with.

Howard August rose from the table. "A smoke, gentlemen?"

"Not tonight, Dad," Kip said, reaching for Jill's hand. "I thought I'd take Jill for a drink and dancing over at the country club."

Jack jumped up. "Oh, that sounds like fun." He grabbed Eleanor's arm. "Why don't we all go?"

"No, thanks," Eleanor said. "I'll just stick around in case J.R. wakes up. He might need something...."

"Howard, Agnes," Jack said, an edge of desperation in his voice, "how about the two of you?"

Agnes seemed reasonably amenable to the idea, but Howard squashed it. "No, no. We'll leave the wining and dancing to the youngsters."

Jack rubbed his hands together. "Well, I guess it'll just be the three of us then," he said, smiling at Kip and Jill.

Kip wasn't about to be outmaneuvered by a stodgy scientist. "Sorry, old man, but my Porsche is a two-seater."

"We can take Jill—*ian's* car."

Kip gave his father a broad wink. "Didn't you have some business stuff you wanted to go over with Harrington this evening, Dad?"

August senior was thrilled to see his son's interest so peaked in Jill and readily agreed. "Besides," August added, putting an avuncular arm around Jack, "you know the old saying—two's company, etc., etc."

Jill gave Jack a wicked smile. The last thing in the world she wanted was a night out on the town with Kipling August, but she felt Jack deserved to stew some more for that humiliating irate brother act he'd pulled up in her room. She slipped her hand through Kip's arm. "Tell J.R. not to wait up for us if you see him to-night, Jack."

"YOU'RE NOT CONCENTRATING, Jack." Howard August gave him a stern look.

"I'm sorry, sir. My head is a little stuffy. Maybe I caught J.R.'s cold." He pretended to fight back a yawn that still managed to escape.

August ignored it and leaned forward in his seat. "So, tell me, Jack, man to man, do you think this spark between Kipling and Jillian will grow into a flame?"

"Spark?" Jack gave August a deliberately blank look.

"Don't tell me you didn't notice?"

"I'm sorry, sir."

"Yes, yes. They're attracted to each other."

"Aren't you . . . jumping the gun a bit, sir? After all, they hardly know each other."

"My son has never been one to waste time in matters of the heart, my boy. And as for Jillian, why, I've never seen her in this flustered, distracted state. If it isn't attraction, what would you call it?"

"Indigestion," Jack muttered.

August chuckled. "Nonsense. I think this is the best thing that could happen to both of them. And I intend to do everything I can to fan the flame, if you get my drift, Harrington."

Jack rose, clutching his stomach. "I meant, sir, that I seem to be having a bout of indigestion." He started backing toward the door. "I'm afraid . . . I really do need . . . to be excused." His hand was on the doorknob. "Could we postpone the rest of this discussion until the morning, sir?"

"I suppose so," August said, giving him a curious look. "This must have been coming on since you arrived here last night. You haven't quite been looking yourself, Harrington."

"I haven't quite been feeling myself, sir," Jack confessed, and with a grateful smile made a quick exit.

He saw Eleanor mounting the stairs. He hurried to catch up with her.

She smiled distractedly at him. "I was just going up to check on J.R."

"Oh. Well, maybe if he's up and feeling better, he might like to go over to the country club."

Eleanor brightened. "Do you think so? After suffering a migraine?"

"Once they go, they go." He gave her a sideways glance. "If I were you, Eleanor, I'd put on a bright evening dress and then go see if J.R. would like to go dancing."

Eleanor wet her lips and gave Jack a quick pat on the back. "Good idea, Jack. Thanks. I've got this great-looking red dress...."

"I bet J.R. will find it irresistible."

She gave him a thoughtful appraisal. "You're all right, Jack."

He grinned.

She winked at him. "And not half bad-looking once you loosen up a bit."

Jack quickly turned the grin into a nerdy grimace. "Why, thank you very much, Eleanor. I'll work on that."

She gave him a look that said he'd have to work very hard, and then tripped gaily off to her room to change into her red dress.

By the time Eleanor knocked on J.R.'s bedroom door, Jack's transformation was complete.

"Why, you look wonderful, J.R.," Eleanor said exuberantly. "You must be feeling better."

"Even better now," Jack said flirtatiously. "That's a dynamite dress, Eleanor."

"Oh, it's just something I had lying around."

He gave her an appraising look. "That's a dress meant for partying." He leaned a little closer to her. "I doubt the Augusts party much."

Eleanor gave a trill laugh. "I've got an idea. Kip and Jillian went over to the country club awhile back. Why don't we drive over and join them? Jillian went in Kip's sports car, so we can use the rental car. We can dance, have a couple of drinks . . ."

"Say no more," Jack said brightly. "Let's blow this joint."

They were at the top of the stairs when Eleanor came to an abrupt halt. "Wait. I should check with Jack Harrington and see if he'd like to join us. He was real eager to go earlier, but Howard wanted to discuss some business with him."

Jack grabbed her arm as she started to turn and head back to Jack's bedroom door.

"I'll check. Why don't you go on down and get our coats?"

Eleanor shrugged. "Okay." But she paused, watching Jack.

He knocked. "Harrington? You awake. It's J.R. Eleanor and I are heading over to the country club. Care to come along?" He pressed his ear to the door, smiling at Eleanor as he pretended to be listening to Jack Harrington's response. He gave Eleanor a little shake of his head.

"Doesn't he want to come?" she called out.

"Indigestion," Jack said, manufacturing a sympathetic nod.

"Wait. I've got some antacids in my room. I'll get them for him." Eleanor took a couple of steps, but Jack held out his hand.

"What's that, Jack?" Pause. "Oh, okay. You sure?" Pause. "See you in the morning then." He returned to Eleanor, took her arm and guided her down the stairs. "He's got antacids. Just took some. He says all he needs is a good night's sleep."

"He's a funny guy, that Harrington," Eleanor mused.

Jack gave her a facetious look. "Not exactly a stand-up comic."

Eleanor tittered. "No, but if he did something more with his appearance, and if he weren't so preoccupied with his work and so socially inept, he'd be . . . almost attractive."

"Well, that's a pretty tall order for the poor guy," Jack said with a sly smile.

Eleanor smiled kittenishly at Jack. She'd been practicing that smile in front of a mirror for days. "Well, all men can't be as fortunate as you, J.R. It's so effortless for you to look good. Very good."

"Oh, there's some effort involved," Jack murmured, flipping a smile back.

"YOU'RE A GREAT DANCER, Jilly." Kip twirled her to a rumba beat around the ample parquet dance floor of the Meadowbrook Country Club.

"I don't dance much," she muttered. *Hardly ever before Tobago. Not at all since. Oh, but on Tobago, she'd danced the night away.*

"It's going to be such fun working together at the foundation," he whispered against her ear as he pulled her closer.

"What about your art, Kip?"

"Ah, art. My father considers art a frivolous diversion."

"I thought you took a certain degree of pride in not thinking like your father."

He laughed softly, directing his warm breath against her ear. "He thinks the world of you, Jilly. And so do I."

"You don't even know me, Kip." This was turning into the longest playing rumba she'd ever heard.

"I plan to get to know you, Jilly. We're going to be seeing a lot of each other from now on."

"You know Kip, there's a firm rule at the foundation that doesn't allow fellow employees to fraternize."

"You needn't worry your pretty little head about that rule, Jilly."

Jill cringed at his condescending words. "I don't think there should be exceptions to the rule, Kip. Besides, some of our other colleagues might object strenuously to your father making an exception."

"Relax, Jilly. It will only be a temporary exception if I have my way," he crooned into her ear.

"You should know, Kip, that my career . . . my position at the foundation . . . is . . . everything to me."

"Then you have some wonderful surprises in store, my sheltered Jilly," Kip said with a devilish smile, maneuvering her into a low dip as he spoke.

As he held her there, his smile slid into a grimace, and for an awful moment Jill thought Kip was going to let go of her.

"Kip . . ." She clutched his jacket sleeve.

"Damn," he muttered, not budging as he stared off in the distance, but thankfully maintaining his grip on her.

Jill let her head drop back, and she got an upside-down view of the source of Kipling August's consternation. She let out a low groan.

Jack caught her eye and waved. So did Eleanor.

Thank goodness the rumba ended, otherwise she might have been held in that dip indefinitely.

"What happened to his migraine?" Kip muttered as the band switched to a slow, romantic fox-trot.

"I guess he recovered." But, Jill wondered, would she?

"He's dancing over here." Kip smiled tightly. "J.R., Eleanor, nice to see you."

Jack smiled back. "You know, Kip, it's been ages since I danced with my sister. Mind if we make a switch?"

Kip clearly minded, as did Eleanor, but both of them recognized that glint of determination and brotherly possessiveness in J.R.'s eyes.

As Jack whirled her off to a far corner of the dance floor, Jill gave him a dark look. "I don't appreciate your constant shadowing, Jack. If you can't trust me . . ."

"It's not that I don't trust you—it's that sweet-talking Casanova. What would you have done if I hadn't walked into your bedroom when I did? Kipper's lips were honing right in on yours."

"Don't call him Kipper, Jack," she snapped.

"I suppose you wanted him to kiss you."

"Really, Jack . . ."

Before she could finish, Kip and Eleanor twirled by. Kip tapped Jack on the shoulder. "May I cut in?"

"No, you may not," Jack muttered under his breath. Fortunately only Jill heard him. She gave him a little shove and glided into Kip's arms, leaving Jack no recourse but to dance with the ever-eager Eleanor.

"Kip's very nice," Eleanor said encouragingly. "And he likes your sister. You should be happy for her, J.R."

"He's wrong for her. All wrong."

"Isn't that up to your sister to decide?"

"She hasn't had much experience with men."

The song ended. Jack, with Eleanor in tow, made a beeline for Jill and Kip.

Kip looked like a man fast losing his patience. "Jilly and I were just about to go into the lounge for drinks."

"Great idea," Jack said cheerily.

Unfortunately the only available tables in the lounge were tables for two. And there wasn't a pair within even hearing distance of each other.

Jack was stuck sitting with Eleanor about twenty feet away from the table where Kip and Jill were sitting. Steaming inside, he sipped a martini as he watched the younger August putting the make on his wife.

"J.R.? Did you hear a word I said?"

"What?" Jack looked distractedly across at Eleanor and then resumed his vigilant watch.

Eleanor followed Jack's gaze. She smiled. "They certainly seem to be hitting it off."

"They certainly do," Jack said between clenched teeth.

Eleanor reached out her hand and squeezed Jack's forearm. "Don't you want to see Jillian find a nice young man and settle down?"

Jack had an answer for that question, but he couldn't give it. Instead, he rose abruptly.

"Where are you going, J.R.?"

"They're playing our song."

"I didn't know we had a song."

"Mine and Jill's."

"You and your sister have a song?" For all her infatuation, Eleanor was beginning to have some serious reservations about J.R. Really, she'd heard of mother fixations. But sister fixations?

"Okay, okay, I'm sorry," Jack said as he tried to maneuver a stiff, very angry Jill around the dance floor. "I know you think I spilt that drink on Kip deliberately, but I swear it was an accident. I was upset. What do you expect? A guy watches another man pawing his wife..."

"He was not pawing me."

"But he wanted to paw you."

"I am close to being at my wit's end, Jack."

"We've just had a bit of a rough time, that's all. Twenty years from now, we'll laugh about this."

"I may never laugh again."

"Sure you will."

"We can't go on like this, Jack. I'm walking a very thin line."

"The weekend's almost over. All you have to do is gently give Kipper the brush-off. Sorry. I meant to say Kip."

"You don't just give the boss's son the brush-off."

"You do if you're married, Jilly."

She looked up at him with a wan expression. "You call this a marriage?"

11

"YOU DON'T LOOK GOOD, Jill." Pause. "I mean you don't look well." Pause. "You look like you might be coming down with...something." Pause. "Are you angry?" Pause. "Yes, of course you're angry."

"It's **no good**, Jack."

"It'll get better."

She left off unpacking and sat down wearily on her bed. "Our marriage is a disaster. A farce. A disastrous farce."

Jack sat down behind her. "I shouldn't have behaved like a jealous idiot this weekend. It's just that I love you so, Jill. It's a new experience. Love. Jealousy. Marriage."

Jill leaned forward, hands hugging her knees, staring at her feet. "You've got to leave, Jack," she said in a voice rich with misery.

Jack sat down beside her. "Leave the foundation?"

Slowly, she lifted her head, her eyes fixing on his. "That, too."

"Jill..."

She rose abruptly as he tried to put his arm around her. "I'm going out...for a walk." She grabbed her coat and threw it on. With her back to him, she said in a pained whisper, "I think you should stay in a hotel tonight, Jack. And tomorrow, you'd better start looking for . . . a place to live."

"Jill, you don't mean that. If you're so dead set on my leaving the foundation, I will."

She pivoted around, a look of expectation in her eyes. "You will?"

"Just give me one year."

"One year? Oh, Jack . . ."

"Listen, Jill, no one would quit a golden job like this so fast, not without a very pressing reason. What pressing reason do I give August? What kind of a letter of recommendation do you think he would give me? How do I explain it to prospective employers? They'd think I was out of my mind to walk out on a job like this in less than a month."

"And I think you're out of your mind to keep it," Jill countered sharply.

"But there's really no problem. Look, we just spent a whole weekend with August and son, and neither of them was the least bit wise to the fact that J. R. Ballard and Jack Harrington were one and the same."

"That was one weekend. Kip's going to be working with us at the foundation. What if, one day, he sees you do something or say something that reminds him of . . . J.R.?"

"He won't. Men like Kip never take serious notice of anyone who doesn't pose a threat to their egos. Jack Harrington is just some drab, straight-arrow drudge. And as for Eleanor . . ."

"It's not only work, Jack."

"Things will calm down, Jill. Just give it a chance."

"I can't. Maybe we each can take just so many chances in life. I think I used all of mine up in Tobago." She hurried toward her bedroom door, but Jack caught up with her before she got there.

"You can't go out in this weather. It's freezing. You'll end up with pneumonia."

"I don't care," she said, struggling in vain to get out of his grasp.

"I don't care that you don't care. I happen to care. And I care..."

"Oh, God, Jack, just pack up all your cares and go!" She stared at him defiantly, trying without luck to ignore the creeping heat in her cheeks and neck.

"I can't go, Jill. I care too much," he whispered, a faint but oh so enticing smile on his face. He was still holding on to her, but now his touch was light, provocative.

She could feel her resistance slipping. She could hear a ragged sound. It turned out to be her own expelled breath. "I should have gone to Orlando on my vacation. Disney World. Mickey Mouse. Donald Duck. Thumbelina," she babbled.

Jack's hands slid to her waist. Jill could feel her muscles start to go rubbery.

"I should never have bought those contact lenses. You never would have noticed me with two brown eyes."

"Yes, I would."

He kissed her softly, taking his time. Jill closed her eyes and, with a soft whisper of unbidden pleasure, threaded her fingers through his thick hair and moved closer to him.

"I should never have gone to Tobago. That was my big mistake...."

Slowly he removed her coat. It swished to the floor. He started on the buttons of her shirt.

"Maybe it was the callaloo. I should have ignored your suggestion and eaten something...ordinary. Something...oh...oh, Jack..."

His lips found hers once again, temporarily ending her ruminations.

"We shouldn't be doing this," she gasped when the kiss finally ended.

"Married folk do this all the time," Jack murmured as he continued undressing her.

"I can't think when you...do that," she said breathlessly as his palms cupped her bare breasts.

"Don't think. Feel. How does it feel, Jill?" He nibbled on her neck as he pulled her skirt down over her hips. Then her slip, her panties. They glided down her legs like hot wax on fresh snow.

She wriggled out of them and then kicked off her shoes. Only her knee-high socks remained. Jack quickly saw to them and then stripped off his own clothes with equal haste, flinging them around the bedroom.

With all the ardor and passionate fire of a swashbuckling pirate, Jack scooped Jill into his muscular embrace, carried her over to the bed, flung her onto it and began ravaging her body.

"I love you," he whispered against her mouth. "Bless contact lenses. Bless callaloo. Bless Tobago." His tongue licked her lips.

Her heart was hammering madly. She pressed her body up against him. She couldn't help herself. In spite of everything in her that said this crazy marriage could never work out and she should stop it now, she could feel the dizzy heat rising like a ribbon of fever from her toes right up to her head. Her head was swimming. She could hardly breathe, the air had suddenly become so rarefied. Hot, tropical air. Pounding surf. "Yes, yes," she murmured as his mouth moved to her breast with eager, burning lips. "Bless Tobago. Wonderful ... oh, yes ... exotic ... mmmmm ..... Tobago ..." Her hands were on his back, pressing, kneading, as she strained against him.

Jack was kissing her again, his lips firm, gentle, demanding, all at once. They moaned a little in unison.

He kissed her eyelids, her cheek, the tip of her nose, her chin, marking each spot with the tip of his tongue. Then, slowly, he slid down her body, his kisses bolder and more erotic. "You taste delicious," he murmured against her stomach. And again, against her thigh. His sure hands massaged and kneaded the muscles in the backs of her legs, then parted them with a gentle, insistent pressure. For a moment she stiffened, but then she let go, her breath quickening as his palms cupped her buttocks, lifting her slightly, as he began caressing her with his mouth.

"Oh, no ... oh, yes, yes ..." she gasped, his tongue setting her on fire. She was overcome with shudders of pleasure, all her pulses hammering.

When he entered her at last, she wanted only to be taken, smothered, satiated. She felt wild with lust, faint with arousal, her mouth dry with desire. There was a roaring in her ears, she was turning to liquid, she was going to melt, explode. She could feel Jack throb with excitement as they both cried out their pleasure. Clinging to each other afterward, they felt like two joined souls washed up on a tropical shore.

They fell asleep in each other's arms. Jack slept the sleep of the contented, but Jill's sleep was punctuated with nightmares. When the alarm went off at six forty-five, Monday morning, Jack rolled over sleepily and reached out for Jill.

When he realized she wasn't there, his eyes sprang open and he sat up like a bolt.

Jill was sitting on the chaise, fully dressed for work, looking every bit the efficient, no-nonsense, no-give, conservative businesswoman, regarding him solemnly. When he met her gaze, her eyes slid off him uneasily.

"What happened last night, Jack..."

"What happened last night, Jill, was ecstasy." He wore an erotic grin. That was all he wore.

She tried hard not to notice. "What happened last night doesn't change anything."

He flung off the covers and swung his legs onto the floor.

Jill felt an unbidden rush of arousal at the sight of Jack's naked body, and quickly dropped her gaze. "Jack, please...get dressed. We've got to settle things."

"I think we'd settle things a lot better if you got undressed and came back to bed." A rakish smile curved his lips.

"No." Despite her calm exterior, her heart was racing wildly, as if she'd just run up several flights of stairs.

She folded her hands in her lap, not so much to maintain a prim, distant image, but because her hands were trembling. "I think we need...a period of...separation. We've been on a nonstep roller coaster ride since we met, and I've . . . got to catch my breath. I can't seem to catch it for very long around you." She was clenching her hands, her fingers turning white. "I still want you to find another place to live."

"Jill . . ."

"I mean it, Jack." She had to fight back tears. "I'm just too confused about everything. I can't think straight. I...I need to bring some order and normalcy back into my life. And if you . . . don't leave, I'm afraid I'll never be normal again."

"Normal isn't such great shakes, Jill," Jack murmured, rising from the bed, stark naked, and starting toward her.

"No, Jack, don't," she said sharply, shutting her eyes. He heard the near panic in her voice, and stopped.

"I love you, Jill."

She opened her eyes, ignoring the tears spilling out. "It was all so impulsive, Jack. I need time to separate reality from fantasy. We need a period of...separation."

Jack threw his hands up in the air in frustration. "All we've had is separation. We've slept together exactly twice since we've been home. Talk about the honeymoon being over...."

"I'm talking about the marriage being over," she half sobbed.

"Because I got a little carried away?"

"A little? A little? I don't even know who you are. I wonder if you know half the time."

"I know I'm your husband."

"When you aren't busy being my brother, or some man at work I'm not allowed to know. This just isn't the way I thought marriage was going to be. We're a . . . closet couple. That's what we are, Jack."

"And what should we do about it? You want to come out of the closet?"

"I want you to get out of the closet and get out of this apartment. You can sleep in the spare room until you find another place to live."

"Okay, okay, if that's what you want, that's the way it will be. But it'll take me a little time to find a place. . . ." If he stalled long enough, maybe she'd change her mind.

"By the end of the week, Jack," she said with conviction, staring down at her clasped hands.

"All right," he said with sad resignation.

"And that will be end of J. R. Ballard," she said quietly. "I'll tell Eleanor that my brother's left town. . . ."

"Because I realized I couldn't live without the girl I love. That's the truth, Jill."

"Please, don't make this any harder on me. At least you can finally stop slipping into phone booths. You can just be Jack Harrington." She hesitated. "An employee at the August Foundation. For the year. Once we're not . . . involved . . . well, I suppose we'll be able to . . . manage . . . at work. It'll feel a little . . . crazy . . . but . . ."

"This is what's crazy, Jill. Leaving you is crazy. You love me. I love you." He strode over to her then and went to grab her.

She couldn't very well avoid his nakedness now, so she shoved him away. "Would you put some clothes on, damn it. This isn't Tobago. This is Philadelphia," she cried out. "People don't walk around stark naked in Philadelphia."

"They do in their own homes," he shouted as she bolted from the room.

"This isn't going to be your home for much longer," she shouted back as she shoved her arms in the sleeves of her coat at the front door.

Jack popped out of the room, still naked as a blue jay. "Fine," he snapped.

He took her breath away, even now. "Fine." Her voice lacked a little in the snap department, but she made up for it with a very snappy slam of the front door.

By the time Jack had gotten dressed, Jill was on her way to the foundation, her romantic memories of Tobago, if not unraveling, definitely fraying at the edges.

"JACK, YOU'VE BEEN LOOKING at apartments for five days now. You manage to have some complaint about every place you see. What about the studio you checked out this morning before work?"

"Mice."

"Mice?" Jill gave him a skeptical look.

Jack smiled innocently. "Really, Jill. Mice." He stretched his hands out showing a good foot-wide spread. "This big."

"Next, you'll be trying to sell me the Liberty Bell."

He grinned. "Well, given that there's a big crack in it, I'd let it go cheap."

"This isn't funny, Jack."

"Okay, okay," he said contritely. "I lied. The mice weren't that big, but what they lacked in size they made up for in numbers."

"Oh, you're impossible." She shook the newspaper open to the real estate section and began going down the list of apartments for rent. "Okay, here's one. A one-bedroom . . ."

He came up behind her. "Which one?"

She read aloud. "Very large, modern one-bedroom apartment. Wall-to-wall carpeting, convenient location. Available immediately."

He leaned a little closer, pretending sudden nearsightedness as he examined the ad, his warm breath deliberately breezing by her ear. "It sounds good, if only . . ."

"If only what?" she snapped. "The rent is reasonable, the location is perfect. It's right on Cherry Street, less than ten minutes from the foundation. Why, you could even walk to work."

"No pets."

"What?"

"Right at the end of the ad. It says no pets allowed."

"I know what it says. You don't have any pets."

"Not yet."

"You never once mentioned wanting a pet. This is just another one of your excuses, Jack. But it's not going to work. You've got exactly two days to find an apartment. Or else you can just camp out in a shelter."

"You're a hard woman, Jill."

"I'm a desperate woman, Jack." She threw down the paper. "J.R. has got to go."

But J.R. was Jack's ace in the hole. If J.R. disappeared, Jack would have no way of getting within a mile of Jill. Except at work. And Jack knew that if he made a move on Jill at the foundation, not only would they both lose their jobs, but Jill would never forgive him and he'd lose her for good. And if that happened, he knew who would move in fast. Kip August.

Kip, who'd joined the foundation that past Monday, was playing it cool enough at work with Jill, but in the past five days he'd called her at least a dozen times at home, and shown up at her door three times so far. Jill was doing her best to keep him at bay, but the real impediment to Kip's amorous pursuit of Jill was brother J.R. And Jack meant to keep it that way. Only, time was running out.

He took up the newspaper and started circling rentals at random, just to calm Jill down.

It seemed to work. "I'm going to put up a steak," she said, heading for the kitchen. "Want one?"

He looked up from the paper. Just as he said, "Sure," the doorbell rang.

He gave her a rueful grimace. "Your new flame, Kip, no doubt."

"Or your new flame, Eleanor," she said snidely.

They were both right.

And as it turned out, Eleanor and Kip turned out to be the answer to Jack's prayers.

"Have you eaten yet?" Eleanor asked Jack.

"I was...just about to put up a...couple of steaks," Jill answered for him. "I'd invite you both, but I don't have extras."

"Never mind," Kip said, stepping into the apartment and putting his hands on Jill's shoulders. "You're not cooking tonight. We're going out for dinner." He winked at Jack. "A double date. To celebrate."

"To celebrate what?" Jack asked warily.

Kip's eyes bore into Jill's. "My new apartment." He smiled seductively at her. "Guess where?"

"Where?" The question came from Jack.

Kip's gaze didn't sway from Jill's face. "Right down the hall. Just think, Jilly, next time you go outside to look at the stars and get locked out on your terrace, you can just sashay down the ledge to my place. I'll be sure to keep the slider to my bedroom unlocked."

Jill shot blabbermouth Eleanor a hard glare, and Jack shot a mean gaze in lecherous Kip's direction, but both Kip and Eleanor continued to beam.

Eleanor took hold of Jack's arm. "I was the one who spotted the apartment for rent in the paper, right after Kip mentioned to me he wanted to move out of his parents' place and into a place right in town."

Jack, unfortunately, hadn't spotted the ad, or he'd have grabbed it in a minute. It was the next best spot to be in, if Jill really meant to kick him out. Now, not only had he missed a golden opportunity, but he was going to have Kip right on Jill's doorstep.

"Kip fell in love with the place the minute he saw it," Eleanor went on.

"I bet he did," Jack muttered.

"Of course, Kip doesn't really need that big an apartment just for himself," Eleanor continued. "So I suggested he get himself a roommate. And Kip thought that was a great idea."

Jack seethed as he watched Kip devouring Jill with his eyes. He knew just who Kip had in mind for his *roommate*.

"What do you say, J.R.?" Eleanor asked with child-like innocence.

"Over my dead body," Jack hissed.

Eleanor looked stunned. And then the light dawned. She grinned at Jill. "With this brother of yours around, Jillian, you certainly never have to worry about your honor being upheld."

Jill had to smile. "You've said a mouthful there, Eleanor."

Eleanor gave Jack's arm a squeeze. "I didn't mean Jillian, J.R., I meant you. I thought you might like to be Kip's roommate. Jillian mentioned to me the other day that you were looking for a place...."

"I told you that J.R. was thinking of moving back to ... Texas," Jill corrected her, flashing Jack a warning glance.

"Well, yes, you did mention that, Jillian," Eleanor agreed, "but maybe J.R. still wants to give ... Philadelphia ... a chance." Her eyes zeroed in on Jack with expectation. "You've only been here for a short time, J.R. Not nearly long enough to discover all ... this city ... has to offer you."

A faint smile crept into Jack's lips, but Jill's mouth was a tight line dipping down at either end. "I don't think *this city* agrees with J.R.," Jill said, her voice, like her mouth, dipping down.

"Well, maybe going back to Texas might be the right thing to do, J.R.," Kip piped in. After all, he'd only considered Eleanor's suggestion of J.R. for a roommate to extricate big brother from Jill's apartment so that he could make his move on her. J.R.'s return clear across the country to Texas suited Kip's interests a lot more than a trip across the hall.

An apartment across the hall with Kipper suited Jack's interests to a tee. He could remain close to Jill and keep the panting painter in tow at the same time. With a congenial smile, he slung a comradely arm around Kip's shoulder. "Texas isn't going anywhere. Eleanor's got a point. I really shouldn't give up on *this city* without giving it a second chance." His eyes twinkled as he cast his smile in Jill's direction. He could almost see the little puffs of smoke escaping her ears, she was so angry.

"What's the matter, Jilly?" Kip asked with concern. "Aren't you happy your brother's still going to be nearby?"

Sure she's happy," Jack said, pinching her cheek. "Just before you showed up, she was reading me the real estate ads trying to find me an apartment in Philly. Isn't that so, Jill?"

Jill's warm brown eyes turned inky dark. How could he do this to her? Where was it all going to end? He was impossible, incorrigible, infuriating, but, she also had to admit, indefatigable. While this whole mad, crazy charade was wearing her down, it seemed only to invigorate Jack all the more. Just look at him. He was rubbing his hands in glee.

"So, Kip, when do you move in across the hall?" Jack asked cheerily.

"I already signed the lease. It's mine right now."

"Great. I can start moving my stuff over there to-morrow. By Sunday, I'll be all settled in." He still had one arm around Kip, and now he put his free arm around Jill, who felt as rigid as a bar of peanut brittle. "So, where shall we go to celebrate?"

"I JUST CAN'T FIGURE your brother out," Eleanor mused, sitting across from Jill in Jill's office.

"You're not the only one," Jill muttered.

"I thought once he got...settled in his own place...he wouldn't be so . . . distracted. He's been there close to two weeks now and he's still edgy. It's that other woman. I know it is. He just can't seem to let her go."

"Has he . . . said anything to you about her since he moved in with Kip?" Jill made an effort to keep her voice casual.

"He's never even spoken her name. He doesn't have to talk about her. She's like a shadow hovering over him, constantly pushing me out of the way. I know he's your brother, Jillian but I think J.R. has an...unhealthy obsession with this woman. He can't live with her, and he can't live without her."

Jill sighed. She knew how Jack felt. She felt exactly the same way.

KIP SLIPPED THE GRANT application back in its folder, then looked over at Jack who was sitting behind his desk going over some notes. "So what do you think, Harrington?"

Jack looked up, fidgeting with his glasses. "About the application? I told you it's too . . ."

"Not the application. Jilly."

"Jillian Ballard? What does she have to do with the grant?"

"She's got nothing to do with the grant. Jeez, Harrington, don't you ever think about anything but work? I want to know whether Jilly ever mentions me to you. Whether you think I'm getting to first base with her."

Jack could feel his fists start to clench. "Isn't it a little soon to be getting to first base?" he said sharply.

Kip laughed dryly. "No one could ever accuse you of being a party animal, Harrington, that's for sure. Haven't you ever . . . you know . . . hit a homerun?" He winked.

Jack dug his tightly clenched hands in his pockets and pursed his lips. "I gather you're not referring to baseball."

Kip grinned. "Baseball isn't my sport of choice."

Jack cleared his throat. "No, I didn't think it was."

Kip leaned back in his chair and stretched out his legs. "If I could just get Jilly to loosen up a little . . ."

"Perhaps you aren't her type," Jack suggested starchly.

"Nah, that's not it. It's that damn brother of hers. I thought once I moved him in with me and got him out of Jill's hair, she would feel a little freer to . . . be herself."

"And she isn't feeling . . . freer?"

"Nah. It's as if he were watching her even when he's not around. She's so afraid he'll think she's misbehaving or something." He sat up fully again, resting his elbows on the desk, and gave Jack a leering smile. "Not that she isn't hungry."

All of Jack's muscles tightened. "Hungry?"

"I'm not talking food here, Harrington," Kip said with a chuckle, oblivious to Jack's barely contained fury. Jack was right when he told Jill men like Kip August were too caught up in themselves to notice anyone but the competition. And August, Jr. most definitely did not see nerdy Jack Harrington as competition.

"She wants a man, Harrington," Kip went on as he rose from his chair. "She needs a man. It would do wonders for her." He smiled conspiratorially at Jack as he got to the door. "And I know just the man for her."

Jack watched Kipling August exit, his eyes glinting with new resolve. "So do I, Kipper," he murmured. "So do I."

12

IF SHE HAD IT to do over again, would she do it differently? That was the question. The problem was, Jill wasn't sure of the answer. All she was sure of was that she was hopelessly confused. She was married, but she wasn't married. She was an only child, but she had a brother. There was a man she worked with that she was supposed to hardly know who happened to be her husband. Since she'd first set eyes on her swashbuckling pirate in Tobago, she'd had no sense of reality at all. And hardly a moment's peace. How long could she go on like this? That was also the question. And Jill had already come up with an answer to that one. Not much longer.

It was Friday afternoon, and Jill had just come home from work. She got undressed and threw on a robe. The house seemed so quiet and empty without Jack. Then again, with him, it had been utter chaos. With some exhilarating doses of passion thrown in.

Could she have solved everything if she, instead of Jack, had agreed to leave her job at the foundation? Was it really only her ambition and what she considered to be the rules of fair play that was keeping her and Jack apart? Was she foolish to let her career stand in the way of true love?

No. It wasn't as simple as that. The issue of her career was certainly one of the conflicts, but it had gone beyond that for Jill. Not only did her whole marriage seem a farce, and not only couldn't she reconcile the many faces of Jack Harrington, but she felt as if she were at constant war with herself. The straitlaced, conventional, methodical Jillian was doing battle with an irrepressible, brazen free spirit within—a lustful, passionate, daring nymph. In Tobago she had been Venus on the half shell. In Philly, she was a clam locked in a shell that even goodly doses of steam couldn't open long enough for her to fully escape. How did two such divergent and antithetical selves exist in one body? Tenuously.

The doorbell rang.

Jill hesitated. The only person she wanted to see was Jack. The only person she couldn't handle seeing was Jack. Her two selves at war.

The doorbell rang again.

She'd have liked to do a disappearing act right there and then, but as instant evaporation wasn't in the cards, she walked resolutely over to the door and opened it.

"Hi, Jilly."

Jill gave Kip a wan smile. "I was just about to take a shower."

"You've always got some excuse for avoiding me, Jilly."

"It's just not . . . right, Kip."

He stepped inside. "What's not right?"

"We shouldn't be . . . socializing."

"Why not? You're not *socializing* with anyone else, are you, Jilly?"

"No, not...at the moment." She gave him a sad, lost look that Kip misinterpreted.

"You've just got to loosen up a little, Jilly. Let yourself experience life. You're really quite attractive. The right man, Jilly, could do wonders for you. If you'd just give me a chance." His hands moved sinuously up the sleeves of her terry robe.

"Kip...don't. I meant we shouldn't socialize because I still don't feel it's right for your father to make us a special exception. We should adhere to company policy just like everyone else. It's only fair."

"Come on, Jilly. One of these days I'll be making the company policy."

"But you aren't making it yet. And...some people at the foundation have been making...snide comments...."

"You won't have to listen to them much longer, Jilly."

Jill gave him a cautious look, oblivious, for the moment, to Kip's fingers caressing her neck and shoulders. "What is that supposed to mean?"

"Just say the word, Jilly."

"The word?"

He took hold of her head and drew her closer. "Say yes, Jilly. Say yes, and you'll never have to work another day in your life. I'll fulfill your every need, darling. Say yes, Jilly, and you'll make me the happiest man in the world."

"You can't...fulfill my needs, Kip. Really, you... can't."

"I love you, Jilly. Isn't true love all any woman truly wants when you get right down to it?"

"Maybe the women you've known before me, Kip. But I..."

"Dad said you were just the type of woman I needed," Kip declared, cutting her off, "and he was right. He wants this as much as I do. So does my mom. She's just waiting for the word and she'll order the invitations."

"The invitations? Kip I'm trying to explain...."

"Oh, Jilly, you'll make such a beautiful bride. With just a few modifications..."

AT THE VERY MOMENT Kip was proposing to Jill, Jack was opening a business-size envelope in his apartment across the hall. When he read the contents his first instinct was to deny what he'd read. A mistake. A ghastly mistake. But he read the letter again, the denial slipping away. He felt at once cold, fevered and dizzy. He sank into a chair, crumpled the piece of stationery with raised letterhead reading Cromwell, Foster and O'Brien, Attorneys at Law, and dropped his head into his hands. Jill had filed for divorce.

Slowly, he regrouped. This was crazy. Jill didn't really want a divorce. She loved him. He loved her. They were meant for each other. He grabbed the crumpled letter from the floor, balled it even smaller, then flung it across the living room.

Okay, he decided, if Jill wanted him to quit the foundation, he'd quit. He'd quit on Monday, the hell with giving it a year. The hell with his career. Without Jill, nothing mattered. He'd quit his job, move back in with his wife, and they'd start again. This time a bit more conventionally. Maybe there was something to be said for convention.

He walked across the hall. There was a spring in his step. It would all work out. *Jack and Jill forever.*

JILL WAS DESPERATELY trying to disentangle herself from Kip's amorous embrace when the doorbell rang.

"Jill. Jill, it's me. Let me in. We've got to talk," Jack called out.

Kip expelled an exasperated sigh. "Give it a rest, J.R.," he shouted. "Your sister and I are talking right now."

Jack banged against the door. "Jill, open up."

Jill shut her eyes, swaying a little. She could tell from the tone of Jack's voice, and from the way he was banging on the door, that he must have received the letter from the divorce lawyer. Damn. It had arrived sooner than she'd expected. She'd planned to tell Jack herself this evening. A divorce seemed her only way out. She just couldn't go on like this anymore.

"Jill. Open this door."

"She's not dressed, J.R. She's about to go into the shower and she's asked me to wash her back," Kip called out, much to Jill's dismay. But as she started to protest and tell Jack it wasn't true, she realized that maybe it was just as well that Jack got the wrong idea. Maybe then he'd accept that a divorce was the only solution.

"Jill? What's happening, Jill?" Panic and anger tangled in Jack's voice.

Kip, having had just about enough of big brother's interference in his pursuit of his true love, replied in a glib, insinuating tone, "Use your imagination, J.R."

The banging on the door and Jack's shouts came to a sudden stop. Jill squeezed her eyes shut and bit down hard on her lower lip. Tears slipped down her closed lids.

Kip saw the stricken look on her face. "Your brother will come around, Jilly," he said soothingly, stroking her hair. "Once he sees that my intentions are honorable . . ."

JACK AND JILL TOOK OFF separately for the weekend, both desperate to escape the City of Brotherly Love, not to mention each other, Kip and Eleanor. Jill headed for New Hope, an artists' mecca in Bucks County. There were fine galleries, quaint shops, boutiques and even a horse-drawn carriage tour of the town, weather permitting. Actually the weather was quite mild that weekend and the carriage tours were in operation. After seeing a half-dozen couples, either hand in hand or arm in arm, boarding the carriages, Jill quickly decided to skip it.

Jack rented a car and drove into the Pennsylvania Dutch region of Lancaster County. The bucolic countryside, dusted with snow, punctuated with one-room school houses, picture-perfect farms and general stores, should have had a soothing effect on Jack's nerves, but didn't.

Just past a quaint little town charmingly named Bird-in-Hand, Jack saw a sign for buggy rides. Maybe a carriage ride down country lanes would perk up his flagging spirits. But when he got to the boarding spot and saw a few families and a handful of happy couples waiting to take a spin, he drove on. He was too miserable to witness the cheery happiness of others.

Jill stayed the night at a charming cream-colored clapboard inn right on the Delaware River. Her luck—just as she was registering, a besotted pair of newlyweds arrived to take up a week-long residence in the honeymoon suite. . . .

Jack opted for the sterile anonymity of a strip motel, just south of Bird-in-Hand. His luck—right next door, separated by a paper-thin wall, was a pair of lovers setting new records. . . .

Jill couldn't sleep. She ended up reading most of the night. A *Wall Street Journal* she found lying on the desk . . .

Jack tossed and turned for hours and finally gave up trying to sleep. He switched on the TV. Sally Jesse Raphael was interviewing five men who liked to wear their wives' clothes. . . .

MONDAY WAS GRAY and gloomy. It fit Jill's mood perfectly. She woke up early, dressed quickly, and left her apartment before dawn's early light. She didn't want either an effervescent Kip or an angry, distraught Jack showing up at her door, suggesting they accompany her to the foundation.

She needn't have worried about Jack making an appearance. Jack headed for the foundation on Monday morning from his motel outside of Bird-in-Hand. He hadn't gone back to the apartment he shared with Kip on Sunday night because he would have only ended up taking a swing at him. He hadn't taken a swing at anyone since the fifth grade. Unfortunately the kid he'd swung at had ducked, and ended up coming back with a right clip to his jaw, knocking him out cold. It had been a humiliating experience, and Jack had no desire to take the risk of repeating the humiliation now of all times.

Jack arrived at work just in time for the staff meeting Howard Wendell August had called for nine that morning. He met up with Jill in the hall as they were both heading for the conference room.

"Good morning, Jillian," he said archly. "Did you have a pleasant weekend?"

Jill merely shrugged. Jack's voice seemed to be coming to her from faraway, another planet, another life.

"Aren't you going to ask me about my weekend, Jillian?"

She felt drained of energy. "How was your weekend, Jack?"

"Miserable."

They looked at each other, and then Jill's eyes dropped as she silently reflected on her own misery. The sad truth was that she still loved Jack desperately and hated being the cause of his pain and fury.

"I was going to tell you, Jack. About . . . seeing a lawyer." She glanced sideways at him. "I'm sorry, Jack." She felt tears brim in her eyes.

"Yeah, I'm sorry, too," he said brusquely, picking up his pace and striding ahead of her into the conference room. Swashbuckling pirates took broken hearts in their stride, didn't they? Then again, his swashbuckling days were coming to a fast end.

Before Jill entered the room, she smoothed her hair back and pulled down the jacket of her gray suit, nervous acts to ensure that she was neat and tidy before parading in front of her associates. Today, the gestures took on added meaning. Maybe if she looked put together on the outside, no one would suspect that on the inside she was becoming completely unglued.

Uncustomarily Jill was the last to arrive. There were a dozen key staff members grouped around the large cherry wood conference table. Jack was sitting close to the window, between two of his assistants. Kip was sitting next to Eleanor, but he'd saved the seat on his other side for Jill. Jill deliberately slipped into an empty seat several chairs away. She glanced over at Howard Wendell August, who sat at the head of the table, observing the group with a measured look of great seriousness.

August greeted the group with typical forced joviality and then cut immediately to business. The August Foundation was expanding, and he, for one, was quite excited about the new creative arts project being headed up by his son. He regarded Kip with a look of pride and pleasure, and then droned on for ten minutes, summarizing the goals of the foundation for the upcoming month.

Jill tried to concentrate on August's platform and made every attempt to avoid looking over at Jack, but she wasn't very successful. Each time she snuck a glance at Jack, he was sitting up straight, rigid in his chair, his face maintaining a hard, impassive expression. Inside, was he suffering the same anguish that was threatening to devour her? she wondered. *Oh, Jack, I wish we had never left Tobago. I wish I really was a wild, exotic island princess. I wish you really were a buccaneer....*

"Now let me give the floor to Kipling," Howard was saying. "And he'll elaborate on his key project proposals."

Kip rose from his seat. He looked around the room, his eyes coming to rest on Jill. He smiled warmly at her. Jill quirked a faint, uneasy smile on and off in response.

"Before I get to business," Kip said, his eyes remaining fixed on Jill, "I have an announcement to make."

Jill took a quick look at Jack. His eyes were glued to Kip.

"I'd like you all as witnesses when I ask the woman I love to marry me," Kip said beaming. "Well, Jilly . . . ?"

Howard August applauded. "Wonderful, wonderful . . ."

Jill sprang out of her seat. "No, no, I can't . . ." she stammered.

Jack turned white. He popped out of his chair, knocking it over. "Can't? I'll say you can't," he screamed at Jill. "You're already married."

"Married? Jillian? Impossible," Howard stated firmly.

"It's true," Jack snapped, having reached his wit's end. "I should know. I'm her husband."

Both August junior and senior stared at Jack in stunned silence. Eleanor's mouth dropped open. Jill sank back into her seat. The rest of the group was agog.

August turned to Jill, observing her incredulously. "This can't be true, Jillian. It's against the rules."

"You can take your rules and . . ." Jack threatened, but before he could finish telling August where to put them, Kip stormed over and made a grab for him. Jack shoved him away, pulled off his glasses, threw down his jacket and put up his fists.

"I've been itching to do this, Kipper, since that first pass you made at my wife." He did a little footwork. "Come on, Kipper. Put up your dukes."

"Jack, stop. This is crazy," Jill pleaded.

Jack dished her a wiseacre grin. Then in a deliberately thick western twang, he murmured, "What's the matter, Jilly? Think he can take me?"

A loud gasp of shock escaped Eleanor's lips as she stared at Jack with wide, disbelieving eyes. "J.R.?"

Kip stumbled back, his eyes fixed on Jack as well. "J.R.?"

Howard August gave Jack a closer scrutiny. "J.R.?"

Eleanor marched over to Jack and pointed an accusatory finger at him. "You can't be...Jillian's husband, J.R. You're...her brother."

"That's right," Kip seconded. "And don't think you really pulled the wool over anyone's eyes, J.R. I knew there was something fishy about you...you and Jack...the whole time."

Howard Wendell August turned his hard gaze on Jack. "Which is it, young man? Are you Jillian's brother or her husband?"

Jack hesitated, casting a rueful gaze at Jill. "I suppose you could say...both."

"Oh," moaned Eleanor, "this is sick. This is so sick." She swayed and fell against Kip's chest. His arms went around her to keep her from sinking to the ground.

"For heaven's sake," Jill snapped, her voice thick with exasperation. "Jack only pretended to be my brother."

Kip, still supporting the limp Eleanor in his arms, gazed at Jill with renewed hope. "Is he only pretending to be your husband as well?"

Jill sighed. "No. That part's real."

Howard Wendell August slammed his fist down on the table. "This is a disgrace. In the entire history of the August Foundation I have never witnessed such a flagrant disregard of the rules. Not to mention that my son and I have been made laughingstocks. I am relieving you both of your service as of this moment. You're fired."

Distraught and furious, Jill leapt back out of her seat and glared at August. "But it was just hunky-dory for your son to flagrantly break your ridiculous, antiquated rules, wasn't it? Why, you're nothing but a pompous hypocrite. And furthermore, I wouldn't marry your son even if . . . I wasn't already married." She turned her glare on everyone in the room, Jack no exception, and fled without another word.

Jack gave Howard Wendell August one last blistering look before taking off after Jill. "And another thing. You can't fire me, you stodgy, antiquated old goat. I already quit. My letter of resignation is sitting on your desk."

Jack grabbed his glasses, but before he put them on, Kip deposited Eleanor in a chair, made a fist and clipped the unprepared Jack in the jaw.

Well, if ever there was a day for humiliation . . .

BY THE TIME JACK got to Jill's apartment, she was gone. He'd run up the stairs, all five flights, and his heart was pounding, his shirt sweaty. He pulled his jacket off, threw it on Jill's bed. It slid to the floor in a heap. He left it there and sank down wearily on the edge of the bed.

Where was she? He had to speak to her. He had to make her see that nothing else mattered but the two of them. *Jack and Jill forever.*

He fell back on the bed, on her pillow. He breathed in deeply. He could smell the warm perfumy scent of her body, an alluring hint of hibiscus and lime.

Where was she? How long would she be gone? What if she simply disappeared into the night and he never saw her again?

He wrenched himself away from that idea, turning his whole body to the side. His eyes fell on an envelope on Jill's bedside table. The flap was open, a folded sheet of paper half pulled out.

It was a brief note. He read it slowly, and as he did, it was as if a weight was being lifted from him. He folded the letter, stuck it back in the envelope and smiled.

"Yes, of course," he said aloud, and as he said the words he could feel hope returning, strength flooding into him. He dashed across the hall, made a call, packed a suitcase, took a quick shower and changed his clothes.

It's going to be all right, he told himself. I know where she is. All I have to do is get to her, put my arms around her, tell her that as long as we're together we'll be fine. Better than fine.

HER FLESH GLEAMED a honey gold, her body lithe and gloriously proportioned, her face perfection itself: high-cheeked, full-mouthed, the eyebrows fine delicate lines arching over warm chocolate eyes. She wore her auburn hair loose over her shoulders, the gentle tropical breeze making the silken strands fall in seductive disarray.

She walked along the water's edge, the rolling waves lapping at her bare feet. Now and then she'd stop, bend gracefully, and pick up a seashell. She'd hold it in the palm of her hand, inspect it closely, and then let it go, continuing on at a slow, leisurely pace.

He loved her walk, the way her hair moved with her. He was captivated by the scent of her fruity perfume as it wafted in the breeze toward him.

A child was running into the water, splashing the island goddess.

"Sorry," the child shouted.

The goddess smiled. Her glorious smile bowled him over.

She was the one. In her presence even the air around him was different—headier, lusher, richer. He was Robinson Crusoe. And she was his Friday.

She was picking up another seashell. Slowly he approached her. Her head turned in his direction, her eyes lifting.

To his delight, she smiled at him, a demure and utterly beguiling smile. *Delight* meant nothing. He was *delirious* with joy. His whole body quivered.

"I've been a complete jackass," he whispered.

She laughed, a rich, full, captivating laugh. "Jackass and Jill, huh?"

He grinned a buccaneer grin. "Forever."

Dizzy with his actual presence, Jill clung to Jack. This was reality. This was what was meant to be. She wrapped her arms around him. His mouth descended. They kissed roughly, eagerly uninhibitedly. Jill felt herself melting, going limp against him.

"How did you know where to find me?" she asked breathlessly.

"Instinct." He smiled tenderly. "And the letter addressed to us from James and Laura Ivory that was sitting on your beside table."

"I had tea with them this afternoon. They were heartbroken about what happened. They said we were already a legend here on Tobago." Jill looked lovingly down at the wedding band Jack had bought from James. "When Laura saw that I was still wearing the ring, she knew I didn't really want the divorce."

"We belong together, Jill." Jack touched his tongue to the palm of her left hand. It tasted of the sea.

At Jack's sensual touch, Jill felt her whole body tingle with excitement and anticipation. She tightened her arms around him. "How many couples get to be a legend in their own time?"

IT WAS A WEEK LATER, the last day of Jack and Jill's impromptu holiday. They were having morning tea at the Ivorys' and James Ivory was laughing heartily as Jack again recounted how he got to be Jill's brother and all the complications that ensued.

"You laugh," the petite, delicate Laura said in her British accent, "but I have an older brother who was terribly overprotective of me. He used to grill all of my boyfriends, follow me and my blokes on dates. Bloody annoying, Andrew was."

Jill smiled. "I definitely prefer Jack as a husband than as a big brother."

Laura poured the tea. "So, now that you've both lost your jobs, what will you do for work when you go back?" she asked them.

Jack bit into another succulent scone, swallowed and shrugged. "Our biggest problem is references. After what happened at the foundation, the only reference August would ever give us would end us up unemployed for good."

"That isn't fair," Laura protested. "What happened had nothing to do with the quality of your work. You both deserve glowing references."

"Not the way August sees it, I'm sure," Jill said. "As he put it, we not only sinned, we made laughingstocks out of him and his precious son." A devilish smile curved her lips. "For it all, it was worth that, anyway."

"We'll make out somehow, Jill," Jack said with his usual optimism.

"Maybe, after some time passes, this prig of a boss of yours will relent," James said. "He can't really mean to destroy your careers over some dumb, old-fashioned rule."

"You don't know Howard Wendell August," Jill said with a sigh. "The only way we'd ever get a decent reference out of him is . . ." She stopped, a frown creasing her forehead. "I can't even think of a way."

"I'd like to give that bloody pompous boss of yours a piece of my mind," Laura muttered.

"Look, we can't honestly blame Howard," Jill pointed out. "Okay, he did bend the rules where his son was concerned, but then he fully expected I'd leave the foundation gladly as soon as Kip and I tied the knot. And as for Howard himself, the man's got a right to subscribe to a strict code of morality. He certainly lives up to it, and he's justified in expecting his employees to follow suit."

"I say the man's still in the Dark Ages," James countered.

"I agree. There's nothing immoral about colleagues becoming lovers," Laura pointed out. "As long as they're both unattached. I grant you, it's different if one or both of the parties is married."

Jack grinned. "I think that was the ultimate disgrace for the virtuous president of the pristine August Foundation. That his own son was actually involved with a married woman." Jack shot Jill an anxious look. "Well, not *actually* involved, right?"

"Definitely right," Jill said with a vampish smile. "One romantic involvement in a lifetime is all I can handle." Her smile drooped a bit. "I need any leftover energy for pounding the pavements."

Jack put a supportive arm around Jill's shoulder. "Don't worry, Jill, now that we're really together, things are bound to look up."

Jill touched his cheek. "Maybe it's this tropical air, darling, but I feel the same way. Howard Wendell August be damned."

James grinned broadly. "I never did care for those self-righteous, holier-than-though types myself."

Laura readily concurred. "Yes, we can't all be perfect, can we?"

"Think of how dull Howard's life must be," Jill mused.

"You can almost feel sorry for the man," Jack said, and then with a sly smile, repeated, "almost."

After a morning at the Ivorys' filled with laughter, good cheer, English tea and delicious scones, the two couples walked along the beach that led back to the Hotel Caribe Reef.

"Well, I guess we should check out," Jack said. "Our plane leaves for Philly in an hour."

Laura gave Jack and Jill hugs. "You will stay in touch?"

James put a bulky arm around the shoulders of his two friends. "Of course they'll stay in touch, woman. And return here on their next holiday. Like Jack says, things will look up for the two of them."

"I'm sure of it," Jill said optimistically, giving James a warm peck on the cheek.

A few minutes later, as Jack and Jill were checking out, an attractive, young, redheaded woman entered the lobby.

Jill squeezed Jack's arm. "Look over there. Isn't that . . . Cynthia Adams?"

"Who?"

"Cynthia Adams. Howard August's pretty young, southern belle secretary."

Jack turned around and caught the eye of the redhead. "Yes, you're right." He smiled at her. Cynthia smiled back, a blank, friendly smile.

Jack leaned closer to Jill. "Hey, I don't think Cynthia recognizes me."

Jill grinned. "I'm not surprised. No one else at the foundation did until you blew your cover." She smiled brightly at Cynthia.

The secretary dished out another blank smile.

"Why, I don't believe she recognizes me, either," Jill reflected merrily.

A low chuckle escaped Jack's throat and his eyes positively sparkled. "Well, well, well, but I bet the fellow heading over toward her will."

Jill's mouth dropped open as she watched a small, dapper sixtyish-year-old man approach Cynthia Adams and kiss her full on the lips.

"Well, well, well, is right," Jill murmured, astonished. "Talk about the pot calling the kettle black."

Howard Wendell August glanced idly around the lobby. When he saw the devastatingly alluring auburn-haired beauty in the sarong-style sundress at the checkout counter, he started to give her a brief wink. And then the luscious beauty popped on her horn-rim glasses. August's flirtatious wink turned into a paroxysm of incredulous blinks as the light of recognition dawned.

Jill waved gayly in Howard's direction. Jack followed suit. Howard Wendell August's face sagged and he broke out into a sickly sweat as he realized he'd been caught cheating on his own rules. And worse. Much worse.

"We should go over and say hello," Jill said, suppressing a giggle.

"Yes, it would be rude not to have a few words with our old employer," Jack concurred, smiling brightly.

As they started across the lobby, Jill murmured to Jack, "You were certainly right, darling. Things are bound to look up."

Jack and Jill
Went up the hill
to fetch a pail of water

And this time
Jack watched his step.... -

MILLION DOLLAR JACKPOT
SWEEPSTAKES RULES & REGULATIONS
NO PURCHASE NECESSARY TO ENTER OR RECEIVE A PRIZE

1. Alternate means of entry: Print your name and address on a 3″ × 5″ piece of plain paper and send to the appropriate address below.

In the U.S.	In Canada
MILLION DOLLAR JACKPOT	MILLION DOLLAR JACKPOT
P.O. Box 1867	P.O. Box 609
3010 Walden Avenue	Fort Erie, Ontario
Buffalo, NY 14269-1867	L2A 5X3

2. To enter the Sweepstakes and join the Reader Service, check off the "YES" box on your Sweepstakes Entry Form and return. If you do not wish to join the Reader Service but wish to enter the Sweepstakes only, check off the "NO" box on your Sweepstakes Entry Form. To qualify for the Extra Bonus prize, scratch off the silver on your Lucky Keys. If the registration numbers match, you are eligible for the Extra Bonus Prize offering. Incomplete entries are ineligible. Torstar Corp. and its affiliates are not responsible for mutilated or unreadable entries or inadvertent printing errors. Mechanically reproduced entries are null and void.

3. Whether you take advantage of this offer or not, on or about April 30, 1992, at the offices of D.L. Blair, Inc., Blair, NE, your sweepstakes numbers will be compared against the list of winning numbers generated at random by the computer. However, prizes will only be awarded to individuals who have entered the Sweepstakes. In the event that all prizes are not claimed, a random drawing will be held from all qualified entries received from March 30, 1990 to March 31, 1992, to award all unclaimed prizes. All cash prizes (Grand to Sixth) will be mailed to winners and are payable by check in U.S. funds. Seventh Prize will be shipped to winners via third-class mail. These prizes are in addition to any free, surprise or mystery gifts that might be offered. Versions of this Sweepstakes with different prizes of approximate equal value may appear at retail outlets or in other mailings by Torstar Corp. and its affiliates.

4. PRIZES: (1) *Grand Prize $1,000,000.00 Annuity; (1) First Prize $25,000.00; (1) Second Prize $10,000.00; (5) Third Prize $5,000.00; (10) Fourth Prize $1,000.00; (100) Fifth Prize $250.00; (2,500) Sixth Prize $10.00; (6,000) **Seventh Prize $12.95 ARV.

   *This presentation offers a Grand Prize of a $1,000,000.00 annuity. Winner will receive $33,333.33 a year for 30 years without interest totalling $1,000,000.00.

   **Seventh Prize: A fully illustrated hardcover book, published by Torstar Corp. Approximate Retail Value of the book is $12.95.

   Entrants may cancel the Reader Service at any time without cost or obligation (see details in Center Insert Card).

5. Extra Bonus! This presentation offers an Extra Bonus Prize valued at $33,000.00 to be awarded in a random drawing from all qualified entries received by March 31, 1992. No purchase necessary to enter or receive a prize. To qualify, see instructions in Center Insert Card. Winner will have the choice of any of the merchandise offered or a $33,000.00 check payable in U.S. funds. All other published rules and regulations apply.

6. This Sweepstakes is being conducted under the supervision of D.L. Blair, Inc. By entering the Sweepstakes, each entrant accepts and agrees to be bound by these rules and the decisions of the judges, which shall be final and binding. Odds of winning the random drawing are dependent upon the number of entries received. Taxes, if any, are the sole responsibility of the winners. Prizes are nontransferable. All entries must be received at the address on the detachable Business Reply Card and must be postmarked no later than 12:00 MIDNIGHT on March 31, 1992. The drawing for all unclaimed Sweepstakes prizes and for the Extra Bonus Prize will take place on May 30, 1992, at 12:00 NOON at the offices of D.L. Blair, Inc., Blair, NE.

7. This offer is open to residents of the U.S., United Kingdom, France and Canada, 18 years or older, except employees and immediate family members of Torstar Corp., its affiliates, subsidiaries and all other agencies, entities and persons connected with the use, marketing or conduct of this Sweepstakes. All Federal, State, Provincial, Municipal and local laws apply. Void wherever prohibited or restricted by law. Any litigation within the Province of Quebec respecting the conduct and awarding of a prize in this publicity contest must be submitted to the Régie des Loteries et Courses du Québec.

8. Winners will be notified by mail and may be required to execute an affidavit of eligibility and release, which must be returned within 14 days after notification or an alternate winner may be selected. Canadian winners will be required to correctly answer an arithmetical, skill-testing question administered by mail, which must be returned within a limited time. Winners consent to the use of their name, photograph and/or likeness for advertising and publicity in conjunction with this and similar promotions without additional compensation.

9. For a list of our major prize winners, send a stamped, self-addressed envelope to: MILLION DOLLAR WINNERS LIST, P.O. Box 4510, Blair, NE 68009. Winners Lists will be supplied after the May 30, 1992 drawing date.

Offer limited to one per household.

Coming Soon

Fashion A Whole New You
in classic romantic style
with a trip for two to Paris
via American Airlines®, a
brand-new Mercury Sable
LS and a $2,000 Fashion
Allowance.

Plus, romantic free gifts* are yours to
Fashion A Whole New You.

From September through November, you can take part in
this exciting opportunity from Harlequin.

Watch for details in September.

* with proofs-of-purchase, plus postage and handling

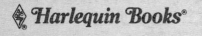 **Harlequin Books®**

HQFW-TS